CARNAGE OF THE REALM

CARNAGE OF THE REALM

CARNAGE OF THE REALM

BY CHARLES A. GOODRUM

CROWN PUBLISHERS, INC., NEW YORK

Inquiries should be addressed to
Crown Publishers, Inc., One Park Avenue,
New York, N.Y. 10016

Printed in the United States of America
Published simultaneously in Canada by
General Publishing Company Limited

Book Design: Shari de Miskey

Library of Congress Cataloging in Publication Data

Goodrum, Charles A

Carnage of the realm.

I. Title.

PZ4.G6563Car [PS3557.059]   813'.5'4   78-27374
ISBN 0-517-53504-1

Second Printing, June, 1979

For
Rita and Buddy Gusack

CARNAGE OF THE REALM

1

EDWARD GEORGE, RECENTLY RETIRED LI-
brarian at Yale, was daydreaming. Strapped in his airline seat,
flickering between thought and sleep, his reverie dwelt upon
computers. His vision had been filled with twitching tape banks.
(Why did they twitch? he asked himself. Why didn't they simply
run smoothly like a tape deck ought to run?) And his eyes sketched
control panels filled with flickering lights. (And that's another
thing. Why *do* they flicker? he brooded. Does anyone really know
what they mean? Is it possible they don't mean a goddamn thing?
Could it be that that was absolutely all there was to them—just
flickering lights attached to nothing at all?) His mind ricocheted
around the problem. What was there about automation that made
it all seem so fraudulent? he asked himself. You'd think that with
all those hard-edged machines they'd be . . . is it possible the
Emperor is actually bare flapping naked at a billion dollars a
minute? What if . . .

1

The plane tilted abruptly and George was jerked to reality with a start. The Washington Monument had suddenly appeared outside his window, and as the pilot banked to approach National from the south George thought, Oh no, not again . . .

George loved to fly—up and flat. He loved takeoffs, he loved cross-country, but he hated landings. Today had been a magnificent fall trip all the way from New Haven—the pilot had taken off with care, studiously avoided even the slightest turbulence for miles—and now he was going to spoil it all with one of those wild charges around the airport. Why do they do this? George asked. His wing dipped even further beneath him, blue sky filled the opposite windows, and then to his surprised delight everything flattened out and the plane went into a graceful glide. With two solid bangs they were down and George was handed back his responsibility. In the air he could leave his life to the pilot, on the ground it was in his own hands and he had no one to blame but himself. He sighed. Edward George liked to be in control of things and of late matters were clearly getting out of hand.

Steve Carson, young friend and graduate student, met him in the lobby. They exchanged clichés, trite but warmly felt, until the bags arrived and the younger man scooped them up and headed for the door.

"Where's Crighton?" George asked.

"She's fighting the traffic out front somewhere. We're to meet her under the TWA sign. She's so anxious to see you she'll be ready to burst."

"She's not half as eager as I am. One of the world's loveliest women. How's your dissertation coming?"

"You had to ask. Goddamn those clothheads! It was rejected. Turned down flat."

"You can't be serious. Surely it was just pro forma."

"No, the nuts are playing tough these days."

"But not with the master work! I can't believe it."

The men neared the curbside with its usual clot of frustrated taxi riders. "Wait a minute," George said. "This is too important to discuss on the run. Let me get settled and I want to hear it from the top. Do you see Crighton?"

A recent triumph of traffic engineering had reduced the airport's traditional chaos to a single lane of creeping, crawling outrage and

Carson said, "There. The brown Audi. She'll be flat out wild."

She could be seen waving frantically from behind the wheel, and as the traffic snailed toward them she pantomimed delight, welcome, frustration, and a few added emotions that were lost in the glare of the windshield, but she finally got within hailing distance and was able to run the repertoire aloud. They got the bags into the trunk, and the older man slipped into the back seat with the young couple in front. Crighton shifted into low and they rejoined the creeping and crawling on the way out of the airport.

"Oh, Mr. George, it is so good to see you!" she said. "When you called, the Werner-Bok practically lit up. The librarian insists you come by tomorrow and even Old Lady Ferrar is excited."

"The feeling is mutual, I assure you—and anyway, I need their help. That's half the reason I'm in Washington."

"Yeah, why *are* you here?" Carson asked.

"Actually an accumulation of things that we'll go into later, but the bottom line is I'm off to London a week from Sunday. What is this? Friday? Will the library be open tomorrow? How about the Library of Congress?"

"Both, I think," Crighton said. "Can we at least have you this evening?"

"You can indeed. We need to catch up. It's been since March, you know."

"Every bit of it. The Carson here has got some kind of a con going that he wants to roll on the way home, but as soon as we get shut of that, it is the vastly expensive meal and a night of gossip."

Carson sighed wearily. "Will you watch your mouth, woman—and your driving. There. Go left. We're headed for Alexandria, Mr. George. It won't take but thirty minutes and then we'll loop back to Washington."

"I am completely at your disposal. What is this 'con' you're accused of?"

They had reached the George Washington Memorial Parkway and sweeping across a landscaped overpass had come down onto the highway and were headed south with the Potomac at their left.

"That's Crighton's idea of humor—but it ties to the thesis." Carson frowned. "The thin-minded jerks. I sent them the finished manuscript in July. It took 'em two months to get off their sabbaticals and then, what with trips to Europe and what-

3

everthehell else five professors can do besides teach, they finally got enough of a quorum to take a vote—and they rejected it unanimously. Philistines."

George smiled benignly. "Surely it's just part of the pageantry."

"It might've been in the old days, but with history Ph.D.'s backed up through six classes, they're weeding like mad. You don't dare take a chance."

"Did they give any specifics?"

"Hah!—more than I'd have thought possible. They must've had help. Most of it was Mickey Mouse, but in one area they have me by the short hair. You recall the thrust of the exercise was in effect a series of questions . . ."

"Wait a minute. We're talking about the frontier, right?"

"Yeah. Mid-1800s. We start with the recognition that people went West—this is American migration. Foreign came later. One, who went? The culls? The misfits? I have proved quite the contrary. There was a natural selection of the aggressive, the innovative, the calm of spirit. Belief in themselves. Then why did they go? If they were such hot stuff, why didn't they stay in their hometowns and get rich? I know the answer to that one too. Finally, what did they do when they reached the empty prairie? Create a Brave New World avoiding all the mistakes of the old? Do it right for a change? No. They re-created a double-distilled reflection of Virginia and Massachusetts down to the last mistake."

They had now reached the edge of Alexandria and George was hurriedly reading a welcome sign, bright, new, and in careful Williamsburg script.

"Seventeen forty-what? Was this really started that far back?" His eyes shifted to the blocks of colonial-style houses, trying to guess which ones were original and which newly planted. "So what is the problem?"

"The problem is, they challenge my evidence, and just because my conclusions run counter to the conventional wisdom, they reject the thesis."

"But you were doing it out of contemporary sources, weren't you? How could they challenge the evidence?"

"Well, to be precise, I guess they challenged my *use* of the evidence. They claim the only validity is what the evidence says. I say it's valid to take the next step—not only what did the letters and the diaries *say,* but *why* did they write them? What were they

4

trying to prove? How did they feel when they wrote them?"

"Ah," said George, " 'legitimate inference—the philosopher's leap from what ought to be to what is."

Carson flushed. "How did you . . . ? I mean, that's exactly . . ."

"Bull's-eye!" Crighton shouted. "You got him in the crosshairs on the first try, Mr. George. Oh, we've needed you around here."

"Shut up, woman," Carson said. "If you didn't have such good legs . . ."

"Break!" George said with a laugh. "We'll pick up the argument later. Why are we in Alexandria?"

"Oh, you'll love this one," Crighton said with wicked delight. "Herodotus here is going to get a medievalist to bail him out of the American frontier."

"A medievalist?"

"Oddly enough, yes," Carson said stiffly. "She happens to be right, for a change. The situation to which Miss Jones alludes comes from a strange passage in a book."

The town had become ever more remorselessly Georgian until there was now nothing but colonial houses, colonial shops, and colonial banks with colonial drive-in windows. Crighton suddenly pulled into the curb beneath a historical sign marking Gadsby's Tavern.

"We're here to move a guy named Vandermann. I'll explain after we get rid of him," Carson said. "I'll be right back." He disappeared around the corner of the building, and George and Crighton were left alone.

"This is very handsome, isn't it?" George said. "I wonder how much of it is real?"

"Quite the majority, I understand. Gadsby's was built before the Revolution and it's exactly as they put it up. Only the woodwork in the ballroom has been replaced—the original was moved to the Metropolitan during the Depression. Over a thousand of the standing houses were actually built in the 1700s. Of course, Alexandria was here some fifty years before Washington was even thought of."

"The town, you mean."

"Yes." She laughed. "The man helped lay the place out, and he had a town house here himself most of his life. He used Gadsby's literally dozens of times."

"You've become quite an expert. How come?"

5

"Too much association with our historian friend, probably. No, I've been giving great thought to buying an apartment or a mews or something here. I'd do it deliberately to link to the traditions, give myself a sense of continuity—'It was going on before you got here, girl, and it'll be running after you're gone'—but I'm not sure it's healthy. Does lived-in history give you peace of mind or an excuse for resignation?"

"Fair question. The British have been struggling with it for years. I find the past fascinating myself, but maybe we're kidding ourselves. Remember Stull Holt's dictum? 'History is a damn dim candle over a damn dark abyss'? There's our historian now. Is he doing all right? How serious is this dissertation thing?"

"I think he's handling it. Of course that's one of the reasons it's so hard to deal with—you can't tell what they're up to. The paper itself is really splendid. If he just survives all this messing around, it ought to give him a real entrée into the profession."

"And his financing?"

"He's solvent, bless his heart. He leaps from one grant to the next. He used to be able to shingle 'em, but things've gotten so tight there's usually a breathless gap between the death of one and the arrival of the next—but he's okay so far. No, his greatest problem is simply outpsyching that dissertation bunch . . ."

Carson had appeared around the building with several men and a single woman who now seized George's attention as firmly as if she had reached into the car and taken his face in her hands. He was quite astonished and thoroughly unprepared for his own reaction. He had not been so moved by a woman's beauty in years. She was about his own age, aristocratic, and stylishly groomed. She was looking directly at him with a pleased smile that seemed to express more satisfaction with herself—something attempted, something done—than recognition. She nodded toward him very slightly, set her look directly into his eyes once more, and then turned toward the other men. The group said its good-byes and separated in various directions, leaving Carson alone with a cheerful-looking man in his early sixties. At one time the man would have been either an abbot or a brewmaster. Now he was simply a plump, bald, college professor with white eyebrows and a red face. The two men slid into the Audi and introductions were made as Crighton drove away from the curb.

"Where am I headed, Dr. Vandermann?" she asked.

6

He replied with a slight Teutonic accent. "Just start down the Parkway toward Mount Vernon," he said. "I live right off the drive about halfway there."

Crighton moved briskly ahead and they made small talk until they were out of the city and driving beside the Potomac again. George shifted the conversation.

"That tavern must be a fascinating place. Were you in the building or did you just come around it?" he asked.

The professor laughed. "No, we were in it. We have rooms on the third floor."

"What's it used for?"

"Well, the first floor is a Williamsburg-type restaurant where they serve colonial food in colonial costume. The waiters are in costume, the food comes on pewter plates. Then the second floor is the eighteenth-century ballroom. It's open like a museum and they give guided tours. The third floor used to be the bedrooms when the tavern was an inn. Now the city rents these out to community groups for good works and cultural activities."

"Which are you?"

He laughed again. "We're cultural. Actually we have a coin club that meets there. We have nearly fifty members now, and I am the president."

"Is that possible! What kinds of coins do you collect?"

"Almost everything, I guess. I specialize in early English hammered—Saxon to Cromwell. Madame Lehman keeps nothing but gold. Poor Mr. Merton collects Victorian heads. Queen Victoria."

"Um," said George. "That sounds more challenging than Indian head pennies. If you'll forgive my saying so, I have always wondered what the appeal of numismatics might be. Collecting dead, corroding coins always struck me as singularly pointless. What should I know?"

Vandermann responded cheerfully. "I suspect the best case that can be made is the fact that coins are about the only way the average man can ever own a true rarity—a true association antique. Most of my coins were struck in the Tower of London, and it is quite likely that William the Conqueror actually touched some of my pieces. There weren't many of them at the time. The odds are in my favor. How else could a salaried man own something touched by a king?"

"That's very good. I'd never thought of that. How did you get involved in the hobby? Do you call it a hobby, by the way—or is it an investment or a . . . ?"

"No, you were right—it is a hobby for most of us. A few do it for the money. I got involved as an aspect of archaeology. It's the simplest way to date a dig, of course. If we excavate a mound and find nothing but Plantagenet coins, we are reasonably certain the building was standing by 1200. Paul Barrow collects Roman silver. There are all kinds of it appearing these days as they dive for sunken ships—scuba diving, you know—all over the Mediterranean. The coins are a very accurate way of determining when a galley went down."

"Of course. That's a whole new thought to me. What is your own field? Are you an archaeologist by trade? No, no, forgive me. Steve said you're a medievalist."

"Yes, I specialize in the Norman conquests up to 1154."

"What happened in 1154?"

"Henry II came to the throne."

Wondering what difference that made, but fearing to learn more about penguins than he wished to know, George veered off in another direction. "I understand Steve here has gotten crosswise to the scholars of your trade. 'How do you use the evidence?' In his period every event is smothered with data. In yours it must be pretty spare. Does that make it easier to handle . . . give you greater control over what you've got . . . or . . ."

"Oh, much harder, sir. You have so little to cross-check it against. Many events of the medieval period are chronicled in just a single place—one lone sentence by one lone monk writing about something that happened a hundred years before his time. Should you believe it? It's all you have. To ignore it leaves a hole of decades! But it's fascinating."

"Then how *do* you check your period?"

"Many ways, of course. Simple common sense works better than you would believe. Jacques Barzun tells a marvelous story about the year 1000 and the end of the world. Do you know it?"

"No . . ."

"Have you ever heard the assertion that as the Christian world approached The Millennium a kind of mass hysteria swept over Europe? People went mad with fear of the coming Judgment Day? That the rich gave their lands to the church and the nobility rushed into monasteries and convents?"

8

"Of course. I heard it again just the other day about our heading for the year 2000. It's traditional. What's wrong with it?"

"A complete myth. Never happened at all. But the history books kept repeating it. Then one day a historian by the name of Burr got to thinking, 'That just doesn't make sense.' One—they didn't even have numbers in those days. They were still using Roman numerals. The year 'M'? Two—they hadn't assigned numbers to years yet. Nobody had any idea how many years it had been since Christ was born and no one much cared. All the chronicles still said things like 'the third year of the reign of Conrad,' or 'the second year after the earthquake at Milan.' Third—no one agreed on when a year started. Was it at Christmas? At Easter and the Resurrection? At the vernal equinox as in Russia or the first of September as in the Greek Empire? A monk wouldn't even think by days of the week— much less by month. To him it was by feast days and fast days before and after a religious holiday.

"So, as Barzun tells it, Burr started working through the written records of his period and finds that no mention of the year 1000 appears in any book printed before about 1700, and the earliest manuscript reference to it is in a text of the late fifteenth century. Contemporary chronicles made no reference to it at all."

"Oh, that's splendid," said George. "Assertion challenged by common sense and checked by contemporary sources. Of course, 'common sense' here is really the man's accumulated knowledge of his field, but still. Do you consider yourself an archaeologist who teaches history for a living or a historian who . . . ?"

"Oh, I hope I'm a historian who applies his knowledge to archaeology." Vandermann appeared to interrupt himself and reflect for a moment, and then he said more slowly, "We all know what *your* field is, sir. You are quite notorious, you know. How unlikely."

"Well, I'd hardly say . . . Have we met before?"

"No. But your involvement in those murders at the Werner-Bok was the talk of the campus. You handled that very skillfully."

"I had a great deal of help—and we were lucky."

"I'm afraid I could use your help in a problem of my own." Vandermann laughed quietly. "That was the Executive Committee of my club back there. One of them has promised to execute *me!*" He laughed again.

"Figuratively speaking, I hope," George said.

9

"No, unfortunately, I think they meant it. Literally, that is."

"Have you told the police?"

"No. It's not that simple. You see, it's someone of whom I am very fond. I . . . tried to solve a puzzle and too late I found out what the answer really meant—and I did not really want to know."

"How distressing—but for your own sake you must . . ."

"No. But I could use some advice. I mean that. Your last experience involved a murder that had already been done—two, in fact, as I recall. Do you suppose you could prevent one from happening?"

Before George could reply, the professor suddenly pointed ahead. "There, Miss . . . If you would just turn off there and then turn immediately into that drive. Yes. And again. Splendid. This is where I live."

Crighton pulled the car into a somewhat cramped half-circle which cut across a surprisingly affluent-looking house. It had the feel of a French country estate pulled forward on a development lot. The street, which was separated from the Parkway by a hundred yards and heavy plantings, had a half-dozen such homes along it, all new, slick-magazine expensive. Crighton thought, Scarcely the scene for a college professor.

Vandermann had the door open and was standing on his graveled drive before George could recapture the dialogue.

"Did I understand you were staying with Mr. Carson, sir?" Vandermann asked.

"No, I stay at the Minerva Club when I'm in town, but I hope to see a good deal of Steve . . ."

"He and I are meeting tomorrow night about his thesis. Is it possible you could come with him?"

"Of course. I'd be delighted to, but . . ."

"Marvelous. Is your paper in that? May I have it?"

Carson lifted an attaché case from between his legs and passed it through the window. "Thank you, sir. I am deeply grateful. When could we come?"

"Eight? Good. I will see you then." He turned and strode with what seemed unnecessary haste into the house.

Carson frowned at George and said, "What . . . ?"

George replied, "I agree. Odd. I wish we knew how seriously to take him."

"Let's go back to town," said Crighton. "It hath been said, 'Never speculate on an empty stomach.' "

"Who said that?" Steve asked.

"I did," she replied and gunned the Audi back onto the Parkway.

2

NELSON, I AM LOOKING BACK ON FORTY years of my working life and fearing I have sold out my profession and my friends. It is a sickening, terrifying feeling, and I find myself rushing from institution to institution to reassure myself that I am wrong. Unfortunately, everywhere I go all I get is confirmation of my doubts and fears."

It was Saturday morning. Nelson Brooks, director of one of the nation's greatest and richest research libraries, was seated behind his vast mahogany desk. Ordinarily Brooks did not go to work on Saturdays, but Edward George's call sounded so troubled that the director insisted on an early and immediate meeting—as much out of curiosity as solicitude. He had been watching his friend closely but merely said, "Like what?"

"It's hard to know where to start, Nelson—or how to condense a thousand hours of spiraled thinking, but let me at least show you the edges.

12

"It's taken me back to my own professional beginnings and I've had to ask myself, how does a librarian justify himself to himself? How do we picture ourselves? I'm convinced there are two kinds of us—the missionaries and the gatherers. The public librarians are in the first bunch and public librarians have only one motivation—they are simply in love with books. Almost any book. They manage to spend a whole lifetime trying to get other people to share their own excitement: 'take a book . . . any book . . . you'll love it . . .' A simple purity.

"Those of us on the research side, though, are quite different. We're in love with knowledge, any knowledge, and to us the end is to gather it in and store it and then get it back when we need it. There's nothing profound about that thought, either. We've been doing it ever since the Nile priests hid the calendar in the basement so they'd be the only ones who knew when the river would rise. But there are two aspects about it that *are* news. One is how much delight it's given people like you and me for three thousand years now, and two, how very good we've been getting at it. We've gone from lists to indexes to bibliographies to catalogs to the computer! We've got the stuff into digital form and can cut back and forth by Boolean logic till hell won't have it. The Millennium at last!"

Brooks looked at his friend. He could not tell if this was slightly irrational hysteria or simply a staged hyperbole. "So, Ed? I'd think you'd be excited with the thought that it came in your time. Jesus, man, you did as much as anyone in the profession to bring it about."

George winced as if he'd been slapped. "Nelson, do you have a computer here?"

"Of course. We're tied to the OCLC net in Ohio and to the Library of Congress's National Union Catalog. We have the New York Times Info Bank, and we do our cataloging on a mini in-house."

"Is the stuff working?"

"Well, yes . . . of course it is. We've had some problems. Much of it's down a good deal and we've had a good bit of human error that's destroyed some records, but I understand we're an exception."

"Who says so?"

Brooks laughed somewhat grimly. "The computer people."

"Exactly. You're not an exception. Everywhere I go I find us getting deeper and deeper into automation and 'little' things are going wrong. Everybody thinks it's just them. Nelson, it's not. The whole profession is in trouble. We always treated our great card catalogs as a sort of joke. We all took them for granted and we let them die. I wonder if the public has any idea of how many of those great tray-filled pieces of furniture haven't had a card added to them in years.

"One institution after another has become the hostage of its main-frames. First the public libraries with their 'book catalogs'—mounds of barely readable printouts—then Toronto in our research field. SUNY. Universities all over the place. Last month the Library of Congress filed its last card—from here on nothing but cathode ray tubes and printouts. And do you know the very first thing that happened when LC did a test run? Almost ten thousand entries were erased in their disk pack! Programming error. They *think* they were able to reconstruct it—but they will never be sure!

"So what difference does it make? I'll tell you what difference—that many books, that many documents, that much of our written experience is taken from us. We're blinded. And you were so right when you said I was at the forefront. Jesus Christ, I must have spent half my energy the last ten years convincing the Ivy League and the Council of Research Libraries that the computer was the way of the future. What have I done, Nelson?"

"Ed, aren't you overreacting here? Are you sure the aberrations that are bugging you aren't just exceptions—anomalies?"

"Answer your own question. When was the last time one of your credit card bills was wrong?"

Brooks laughed. "Last month my water bill and my American Express were both screwed up! You've got me there, but it's only occasionally."

"No it isn't. It's happening everywhere. All-pervasive. When was the last time they couldn't confirm your airplane reservation? 'The computer was down.' When was the last time you couldn't get your bank balance—'the printout got hung up last night.' When were the evening traffic lights out of sync? The checkout registers malfunctioning? All of them computerized and I'll bet everything I said has happened to you within days, not weeks or months ago."

Brooks nodded ruefully. "It's true. What is really odd is the way I've accepted it. When I get a busy signal or a typewriter jams, I bitch all over the place!"

"Exactly. Very odd. But in our profession, Nelson, if our ability to record and store and retrieve for use is lost or eroded, we lose our sole reason for existence. It is fundamental to our trade."

"Um," said Brooks, "you are taking this seriously, aren't you? So what are you doing about it? What are you looking for?"

"I don't know yet. I'm groping. The British Library Association asked me to come over and run a three-day seminar on the computerization of libraries in America. I was on top of our developments when I retired, but in the year since I quit I thought I might have missed out on some innovations so I started calling around casually and found two things: one, that everybody is really committed to automation—all the big libraries are up to their armpits in it. And two: that it's not working right anywhere but that everyone assumes they're the exception and it will all sort itself out any day now. With cards and indexes we were good. We knew what we were doing. Now? Dear God, I'm not sure . . ."

"So how are you proceeding?"

"I want to talk to as many people as I can as quickly as I can before I leave for England Saturday. Who all's automated here in Washington?"

"Hell, practically everybody. D.C. Public, National Library of Medicine, Agriculture. Library of Congress is the local center, but almost everyone is tied to Lockheed and to OCLC in Columbus. State and The Agency are totally computerized!"

"Good. For my purposes that's great. I'm going to start working my way around and see if I can get a pattern. Can I talk to someone here?"

"Sure. I'll have Mrs. Ferrar take you to Fred Currin. He runs the overall setup, though the terminals are everywhere—we input in Cataloging, retrieve in Reference, pay in Payroll . . ."

"Reference. That reminds me. I'm supposed to see a Professor Vandermann tonight. I want to run the Who's Whos on him before I go. Do you know him? He's at Georgetown University."

"No. The name means nothing to me."

"I'll have Crighton take me up to Reference."

"Ed," Brooks said, sensing the conversation was nearing an end, "I don't quite share your concern here, but I'm willing to be shown. If you find anything fundamental in my own shop, you will tell me, won't you?"

"I'll do better than that. I'm going to use you as the symbolic peasant who doesn't know the end of the world is upon him." He stood up and started for the door, smiling. "These are perilous times. Now all I've got to do is prove it so I can spread my despair. I shall return!"

He laughed and headed for the hall thinking to himself, And the worst question is, Should we even be concerned at the loss of bits of data? Might not forgetting clear the way to *new* thoughts and new solutions and is therefore good, or does it keep us exploring the old ways and remaking the old mistakes and is therefore bad? And then there's Steve's problem—how to use what facts we have. He shook his head, sighed, and pushed the elevator button.

By eight o'clock that night George and Carson were on the Parkway just below Alexandria, almost on schedule. The fall evening was clear, sharp dark, and the Potomac sparkled in the night picking up tiny lights from the Maryland shore. Crighton's Audi hummed in a businesslike fashion, and Carson eased back in the seat with a rising sense of well-being. This might all work out yet.

"Did you find anything on Vandermann?" he asked.

"Yes," George replied, "he is both respected and documented! The latter is the important point for a librarian. It makes no difference how impressive a person is; unless someone records his dignity in print, he disappears from our ken like a ship in the night. Vandermann is in print. How did you meet him in the first place?"

"Serendipity, I . . ."

"Have you had courses from him?"

"Nope. Yesterday was the first time I ever laid eyes on him. The whole thing is unlikely. I was reading completely out of my field—I was waiting for a friend and saw a copy of Cantor's *The Life and Death of a Civilization* lying on his desk. I asked if I could borrow it overnight just to clean out some cobwebs, and right in the midst of my despair over the fool thesis I came on this passage that seemed like Providence was trying to Tell Me Something. That's it beside you on the seat. I thought you'd want to take it home, but maybe you can read it by the dome light."

Carson switched on the overhead and George opened the book at an index card that was showing above the pages.

"Here's the picture," Carson said. "Cantor is worrying with the Irish culture of about 600. Europe is absolutely in the darkest of the Dark Ages. The British are still running around naked and

16

painting themselves blue, yet at precisely the same time the Irish have libraries and schools and are writing encyclopedias. How come? Cantor asks. How come the Irish are clear to hell-and-gone away from Rome—hardly any of 'em had even seen the place—yet they are more cultured and better Romans than the Romans are. That's Cantor's answer you've got there."

George tried the page in different directions until he got the best of what little light there was and read with difficulty:

> This can be explained as a manifestation of what may be termed the colonial phenomenon in world history. The people on the fringes of an empire or civilization, the frontiersmen or colonials, are frequently the greatest partisans of the system or culture to which they choose to belong. By their hothouse enthusiasm, their conscious efforts at identification with the civilization whose center is so far away, they make their claim to equal citizenship with the people in the heartland of the civilization. The latter often take their world for granted and do little to perpetuate or improve it.

He closed the book on his finger.

"How about that?" Carson asked. "Does it grab you?"

"Well, it seems to make sense. You're going to claim it makes the frontier conservative. That should flip Turner in his grave. You'd have us believe the pioneers were guardians of the old regime instead of inventors of the new?"

"Exactly! I love it! If I drive myself, I think I can rewrite the dissertation around this theme and have it done by the deadline. Same data; new conclusion."

"Um. Where does Vandermann fit in?"

"That's the weird thing. After I'd read that paragraph, I began to run footnotes and bibliographies to see if the explanation was common knowledge to everyone but me or was it something Cantor thought up by himself. It turned out that all the references either kick back to Cantor alone or to a bird named Vandermann. Cantor is at Brandeis, but Vandermann turns out to be right here at Georgetown. I ran him to earth at that coin club of his and he agreed to read the thesis and talk to me. *Ergo cumquat sum.*"

George was wondering if all this justified Carson's excitement when Carson asked, "What did you find out about him?"

"Well, let's see what I can remember. He wasn't in *Who's Who in America,* but he did make *Who's Who in the Social Sciences.* He was educated in Europe—Holland first, then England, finally the doctorate and graduate work in Germany. He taught in Germany, came here in the early sixties, started at Fordham, and came to Georgetown in the early seventies. No evidence of having been married or having children."

"Very impressive—your memory. Not Vandermann! Anything else?"

"Yes, I tried a few of the European biographical directories and he turned up in several. There was something unusual there by the way that you might find useful in your own research. It's an old librarian's trick. You know these Who's Who things come out every year or so, and unless you think about it, you'll always assume they're cumulative—look in the last one, it'll have everything along the way added up."

"Won't it? You're right, I always ask for the latest edition."

"No, that's how you pick up discontinuities . . . fault lines. All those things are based on filled-out forms—forms sent out by the publisher and filled in by the biographee. If someone is fired or demoted or his 'work in progress' gets aborted, the biographee will usually drop the failure and smooth out the career description the next time he sends in his sheet. Vandermann has a bunch of discontinuities."

"The hell you say. Aren't you obligated to tell the whole story in a Who's Who paragraph?"

"Obligated to whom or by what? It's not an affidavit. No, you can put in anything you want. About the only constraint is not to get so far from the truth that you're vulnerable to ridicule by your peers—in fact, if you're really important, it's considered stylish 'just to hit the high spots.' That way you can bury failures and blind alleys and look modest at the same time!"

"That's amazing. But do libraries keep outdated . . . superseded . . . directories?"

"Libraries keep everything. Sometimes they can't find them, but they keep them."

"My God."

"Yes. Well, Herr Vandermann apparently started out as a journalist specializing in foreign currencies, gold flow, and trade balances. Conservative, anti-Marxist. He seems to have been quite respected in this area in the early post–World War II period and then suddenly he becomes a history professor and in about two

18

editions—four years—all mention of his previous skills disappears, never to be heard of again. From there on he emphasizes his historical interests—and these seem to be going backward too."

"Is that stuff in the Who's Whos?"

"No, you can see that from the card catalog and the magazine indexes. His books and articles. He started writing about the Walloons, then the Tudors, then William the Conqueror, and now all his papers are pre-Saxon!"

"All? Is he that prolific?"

"He gets three or four things published every year and they're retreating about a century a topic."

"Amazing! I must ask him how he does it. We must be about there. These turnoffs all look alike. Do you see anything familiar?"

George did not answer and they drove in silence for several minutes, both looking off the Parkway—which was unlighted and gave the impression of a country road rather than a major artery through one of the densest pieces of suburbia in the nation.

They both discovered the proper access road simultaneously and congratulated themselves as they turned off the main road and started down the narrower pavement.

"Be careful." Crighton had to turn very quickly. "There."

"Got you," Carson said.

He swung left and the car lights swept the length of the house, which was itself lit like a party was in progress in every room. The headlights came to rest on a single car parked in the center of the abbreviated drive. Carson was maneuvering the Audi carefully around the half-circle when the door of the house burst open and a strange, bullet-headed figure ran out and sprinted toward the parked car. The figure was silhouetted against the hall light of the house, so it was a featureless, dull black outline, but the Audi's lights were now focused on the car itself, which to Carson's surprise proved to be a brilliant, metallic purple paint job with painted flames licking around both fenders and over the trunk.

"What the jolly hell?" Carson said, and began to open his door.

The figure was now in the headlights and could be seen as a hatless head made grotesque by a tightly fitting, knotted, woman's stocking. The body was covered by formless, oversized coveralls. It looked toward the Audi, raised two clenched fists in a triumphant gesture, and shrieked something that could have been a foreign phrase pitched in a strange falsetto. The figure jumped into the

19

sports car, spun out the drive, and disappeared behind the plantings of the Parkway.

Carson shouted, "Something's goddamn wrong here. I'll check."

"Be careful. You don't know what's happened. Don't go charging in."

"Right," Carson shouted over his shoulder, halfway to the house.

Carson reached the open door and veered abruptly to the side, half-crouched and peering gingerly around the frame. He suddenly thought of how he must look and thought a bit sheepishly that he had been so conditioned by television he was assuming the classic be-careful-they-may-be-armed stance without a second thought. The house was perfectly silent, but brilliantly lit. He leaned more broadly into the entrance hall and looked around.

There was no one there, but the floor carried neat piles of silverware and silver plate. There were large serving spoons and forks in ordered rows, closed boxes apparently filled with tableware, and a startling number of trays, coffeepots, creamers, and silver bowls. The various piles were lined on either side of the natural pathway out the door as if they had been stacked for collection and transport by prearranged plan.

Carson slipped quietly into the hall and listened. Still nothing. A graceful staircase went up before him, the kitchen seemed to be at the back, and he presumed the two rooms on either side were the dining and living rooms. A larger archway appeared on the right so he peered around its side and found it was indeed the parlor—expensively furnished but devoid of people. A smaller arch with twin doors was across the room by the fireplace and he slipped as quietly as possible toward it. Leaning slowly into the gap made by the half-open doors, he established the room as a study with book-lined walls, a large desk—and dead center in the room a large, half-round desk chair in which Karl Vandermann was sitting with his back to the door. His hands were handcuffed behind him and Carson rushed in shouting, "I'm here! Are you all right? Dr. Vander . . ." By the time he reached the front he knew where he stood. Vandermann was slumped forward, shot precisely in the center of his forehead.

Carson stared at the man, stunned, and then pulled himself together. To his later embarrassment, his first thought had been of himself. "Oh no," his mind had said, "not now, any time but now."

20

3

KARL VANDERMANN'S BODY HAD BEEN DIS-
covered on Saturday night. The Werner-Bok Library did not
normally open until eleven on Sunday mornings––and then only
the exhibit areas, book service began at one—but it was sufficient
delay to nettle Edward George. He was getting too many unre-
solved problems and too little time to deal with them. Snarl and
fume, he said to himself as he approached the guard who was
pushing back the great bronze doors. The officer was programmed
to do three things only: open the building, watch tourists, and
prevent smash-and-grab attacks on the rarity cases. It thus took
longer than would have been expected to get him to call Crighton's
office and announce an out-of-hours visitor, but once alerted, she
dashed up, reassured officialdom, and carried George away. He
followed her down one flight of stairs, through three corridors, and
into an open door marked *Public Relations Officer*. She dropped into

her own desk chair and George eased into the only other one in the small room.

"Hi," she said.

"Hello." He shook his head irritably. "Trouble in River City."

"So I hear. You do seem to attract more than your share. You also seem more bugged than I'm used to for you. Where is the detached observer of the passing parade that we've come to know and love?"

George smiled in spite of himself. "Oh, Crighton, I'm irritated with me. I don't know how to deal with this. That man— Vandermann—asked for our help, but before we could even hear his story, he's taken. I don't have time to make a great thing of it, but I can't tolerate irresolution. It simply is not my affair and I will not be seduced, but . . ." He gestured an exasperated plea. "Have you heard from Steve?"

"He called last night after he'd dropped you off, and gave me the main theme. It is beyond belief. He phoned again about half an hour ago and he's on his way here now. The phone was ringing when I came in. Apparently he had to go back to the courthouse. What is that down there? Fairfax County? Is that where the police station is?"

"It is, and we spent a good part of our lives there last night. Once the police got to Vandermann's house, we went through all the questions five times over, and then we had to follow everybody back to the courthouse and go through them all over again there. Since all I was doing was corroborating Steve, they finished with me but he had to go back this morning and meet some detective . . . a new one. Day shift, apparently. It really is very distressing."

"Did you . . . go into the house?"

"You mean, did I see the body? Yes, I'm afraid so. We all looked at everything. Crighton," he said intently, "it was a very strange scene. Everything was so precisely neat and perfect. Not the slightest sign of hurry or confusion. The silver was perfectly set down on the floor. The chair Vandermann was in was precisely in place at the desk. The bullet hole was exactly in the center of his forehead. A total absence of improvisation or violence. Extraordinary!"

"Steve mentioned the silver, but it wasn't quite clear. It was table silver—not the coins we'd heard about?"

"That was another odd thing. Everything in sight was sterling or plate—and an astonishing amount of it. Almost like a museum, but there was no evidence of the coins at all. Then well into the evening we discovered that the box on his desk—which looked like some kind of paper file—held little flat drawers full of his coins! Every drawer was about so thick—just a little fatter than, say, a silver dollar would be, and all of them had little velvet-lined cutouts with a single coin in each of the circles—dozens of them! Apparently the thief hadn't even noticed them. All he'd seen were the trays and bowls and tableware. Highly ironic."

They looked at each other in silence for a moment and then George said suddenly, "Crighton, you're growing into a beautiful woman."

She looked surprised and said, "Why thank you, sir. I'm a bit more at ease with myself than when we first met. Maybe it shows."

"It may be that, but my advanced age permits me to note that you are also extraordinarily attractive as you march into matronhood. What are you? All of twenty-six?"

"Just that."

"Are you enjoying the work?"

"I am. I've been accepted by the library staff, I think, and it's great fun telling the library's story. We've gotten some beautiful spreads in the slicks recently and everybody's pleased with me. I'm pleased with myself, I guess."

"Good." George abandoned the topic with his characteristic habit of bursting in and out of subjects and proceeded to stare into space.

"Crighton," he began, when the hall outside began to fill with outrage and Steve Carson rolled into the room shouting at a guard for some fundamental violation of his civil rights. Through the barrage of words, Crighton determined that the issue was simply: Carson wanted to come downstairs and the guard didn't want him to. She finally got Carson sitting on the desk, the guard placated and dismissed, and order restored.

With quiet beginning to settle, she grabbed at the top of her head and said, "A simple phone call would have spared us . . . no, forget it. What the hell is going on? Did you learn anything we didn't already know?"

"Yes, Steve, where do we stand?" George asked.

"It's a real can of mixed blessings," Carson said. "I've been thrashing around with the cops down there, and to my embarrassment I can't much blame 'em for the flack they're giving me! They keep trying to brush it all off, and I keep wanting to say, 'It's not as simple as you think,' but every time I get set to argue I think, 'No, dammit, you haven't got time to make a big deal of this!' and my noble rage gets corked back up! Here's the scene:

"I told 'em all about the threat Vandermann laid on us, but the cops say he never had a chance to get knocked off in such style. This was simply a house burglary, they've been getting silver robberies all over the county, and don't get all worked up about it . . .

"The fact is, dammit, it's quite likely they're right—that that is precisely what happened and if we go messing around we'll end up getting some poor innocent in trouble—and waste a hell of a lot of time at least *I* don't have doing it."

"I quite agree," George said. "The difficulty is, we're still caught with the fear that someone may be getting away with murder—oops, an inadvertent literality. But I don't have the time to waste on it either! I know precisely what you mean."

"Look," said Crighton, "why don't you call Lieutenant Conrad and lay the whole shmeer on him. He thinks you're the greatest thing since sliced bread from the last time, and you can unload the whole thing with a clear conscience."

"I tried a version of that myself, but it has problems," George replied. "First, his jurisdiction is limited to the District of Columbia and these officers are exceedingly jealous of their own territories—but more important, he's out of town, can't be reached, and won't be back until tomorrow night."

"Ouch," said Crighton.

At this point the phone went off and everyone jumped.

Crighton lifted it and said, "Press office, may I help?" She looked surprised and said, "It's for you—it's a woman!"

"Thank you," George said, and then *sotto voce,* "I left your number at the Minerva Club in case Steve called." He pointed at the receiver and whispered, "I can't imagine . . . Good morning," he said aloud, "this is Edward George."

"Good morning, sir. My name is Alexa Lehman. You have never heard of me, so don't try to recapture an acquaintance."

The woman on the phone had an accent very similar to Vandermann's, George thought, but on her it sounded better. He felt the voice was slightly Marlene Dietrich but gentler and with a softer sense of humor.

"Actually, ma'am, I *have* heard the name before, I think, but I can't remember where. Where might we . . ."

"No. I am calling you because of Karl Vandermann's death. I am in that coin club of his—and actually I knew him from Germany too."

"Of course! You're the gold lady. Vandermann mentioned you when we met him."

" 'The gold lady!' How . . . well I'm not quite sure! I started to say 'romantic,' but I guess I should know the context first. No, Dr. George, I am calling about the murder. Karl had told me he was going to ask for your help. May I ask, did you have a chance to talk to him or was . . . ?"

"No, I am distressed to say we were on the way to see him when . . . it happened. Do you know what he was concerned about?"

"Only in general, but I do know some details, and others on the Executive Committee know others—and we are eager . . . anxious . . . to tell you what we know. Karl obviously trusted you and we want to talk to you."

George's memory brought up an unusually vivid picture of the woman on the sidewalk and he wondered if this could be she. The voice sounded cultured, poised, and startlingly appealing considering how little he had to work from. It would fit the image.

George sighed and shifted the receiver to his other hand. "Ms. Lehman, I too am deeply concerned about the matter, but I am sorry to say I am leaving the country in a few days, and I simply cannot . . . I have no time I can spare. I am embarrassed to sound so callous, but . . ."

"Dr. George," the woman broke in gently, "I completely sympathize with how this must sound to you. But this is very important to a few of us. I plead with you to give us just one meeting to tell you what we know. After that, we will accept your decision without protest. If the Committee will meet in the room at Gadsby's, will you come . . . please, for just an hour?"

George moved the receiver back. "What can I say? When did you have in mind?"

"Quickly, if possible. Is two o'clock too soon?"

George recalled that Vandermann believed it was one of the Committee who was going to kill him. He wondered if the woman knew this—indeed what *did* she know? He suddenly thought with a chill, maybe that was the real purpose of the meeting—the group wished to find out how much *he* knew. What if they all knew everything and wanted to . . . He shuddered and said, "I think that

25

could be done. Professor Vandermann had actually been talking with a friend of mine. Possibly they exchanged some information that would be appropriate. Could I bring him with me?"

"Of course, whatever you think best. In fact, if he had spoken to Karl in the past few days, we would be eager . . . he might be very useful. Please bring him. You do know where Gadsby's is? Of course, you do. We are on the third floor. The entry is on the side. We will meet you there at two."

They said their good-byes, and George replaced the telephone as Carson shouted, "What are you doing to me? I'm due in Madison a week from Monday! I'm supposed to have a completely rebuilt dissertation in my hand, which I've hardly started, and if I blow it, four years of work goes down the drain. What? What?"

"Yes, I know that, and tell me, what is your *real* problem?"

"My real problem is I'm caught between two rocks and my soft place. If we let the Vandermann thing hang like this, I can't concentrate—all I do is spin it round and round in my mind—and I simply cannot afford the time it will take to get it unstuck."

"Precisely," George said firmly, "and I think I have a time-effective solution. It struck me as that woman was talking. How does this sound to both of you?"

He looked up at the ceiling and began to summarize didactically:

"Situation: One, a combination of guilt, distraction, and curiosity has so seized us that we are unable to do the things this week we must. Two, we cannot release our minds until we have some resolution of our unease—was Professor Vandermann killed in clumsy greed by a stranger or was it sophisticated execution by a friend? Three, we should be able to determine this quickly, at least to the level of our own satisfaction. Four, if we think the crime is indeed linked to the coin club, we can pass what we have learned over to Conrad on Tuesday and wash our hands of the affair. If we are convinced it was simply raw theft and casual murder, we will have released our minds to get on to what should have been occupying them all along. Can you stand to lose forty-eight hours? No more and maybe less?"

"Forty-eight hours . . . two days. Yes, but what makes you think we can learn anything that quickly?"

"We can, I'm sure we can. For one thing, we've got one of the greatest libraries in the world over our heads, and properly played, it will work wonders—but even more, if Nelson will give me access to his computer bases, not only can we break this thing, I can test those infernal machines in a Boolean mode." He was sitting straight upright in his chair and his eyes were glistening. "Forty-eight hours. I know we can do it. Evidence! I'll find it and you interpret it, Steve. Retrieval and interpretation! We can test both our problems in a single pilot study. I like it. What do you think? What do you say?"

Steve grinned and spread his hands. "I am strongly dubious, sir, but hell, I'm useless to anybody in my present condition. Where do we begin?"

"Crighton," George asked, "are you game? We'll try to keep your time consumption to a minimum, but we'll need your intelligence to spot shortcuts. I think you think faster than either of us and if this is going to work we're going to have to function with precision and speed."

"I love it! Roll it, Mr. George! We just wasted two minutes. Forty-seven hours and whatever to go!"

They laughed together, but there was a metallic edge to their laughter. One hundred and twenty-five years of cumulated education and experience were about to lock together in a test and application mode. As an Anglican pope had said, a little learning can be dangerous as hell.

27

4

GEORGE STOOD ON THE CURB AND LOOKED
up reflectively at Gadsby's third floor. His first thought was, They keep talking about the third-floor rooms of the inn, but the building actually has four floors with dormers in the roof; what's up there? His second thought was, Should I walk up that many stairs . . . and then again why not? There's nothing wrong with my heart and it ought to be good exercise.

Carson asked tentatively, "Should you . . . ?"

"Yes," George snapped, and marched firmly into the pedimented doorway. Somewhat embarrassed by his own abruptness, he asked, "You would have us believe that this very staircase held the Founding Fathers?"

"These very boards," Carson said.

"Like who?" George was proceeding rather deliberately up the first flight and marching around a banistered landing heading for the next level.

28

"Hell, everybody you ever heard of. Washington, Jefferson, the Adamses—they all turn up in the guest books. The registers show Hamilton and Burr and Franklin. Remember your coach stops: coming south out of New York the first night was Princeton, second night Philly, third night Dover . . . Coming up from Williamsburg, first night was Fredericksburg, Alexandria was the second, Baltimore the third—the ferry between Maryland and Virginia ran from the bottom of the street out there."

"Ummm," said George, whose breath was barely changing, but whose pace was considerably slowed. He looked up to see The Woman from the Sidewalk waiting at the head of the stairs. George felt a surge of pleasure at her appearance and he smiled at himself. He hadn't responded to a woman so in twenty years. "Oh, to be seventy again." Hell, he thought, he was *just* seventy and by God, she *was* handsome.

"Hello!" she said. "I'm Alexa Lehman. Thank you so much for coming. Our rooms are down this way."

She led them all down the hall and turned into a brightly lit colonial room George thought must have held a dozen beds in its day and clearly would have been more of a dormitory than a "room" in the modern sense. It was now furnished with felt-covered tables, bow chairs, and candlestands, and looked like the second floor of Independence Hall.

There were two men standing to meet them, and the woman's slightly accented contralto organized the introductions smoothly but with unchallengeable control. They seated themselves around the central table and the woman said, "Dr. George, I know how pressed you are for time, so we will dispense with the civilities, and try to pass as much information to you as possible as quickly as we can."

"Ms. Lehman, I cannot believe you could be uncivil if you tried, but let's say we will save the civilities for some other time. Thank you. What should we know?"

The lady smiled with obvious pleasure at the situation and bowed. "Gracefully put, sir. First, let's get our labels sorted out. I am firmly not a 'Ms.' My husband was killed before World War II when we were both very young. I have been referred to as 'Madame Lehman' ever since, which gives me the very best of both worlds. I want to be treated like a woman of Edwardian times, but I consider myself every bit your equal. I expect you to rise when I come into

29

the room, open doors, and seat me at tables, but the moment our minds meet, I will resent it bitterly if you imply in any way that I am a woman." There was a slight twinkle throughout this dictum that took the edge off for George but failed to charm Carson. Crighton was watching as if someone had lifted the glass off a new insect.

"We are the Executive Committee of Karl's coin club. There are normally six of us. Karl is gone, and we are missing two, Jerry Merton and Eleanor York, who will be along any moment now. Again, to go right to the heart of the matter, we think Karl was murdered. It was done deliberately, it was planned, and he knew it was coming. We believe that someone must do something and do it quickly to see that whoever did it is caught, that justice is meted out, and that he does not murder again. We have heard that the police think Karl's death was a by-product of a robbery, and we believe that this explanation is false and dangerous."

George looked at the two men at the table. "Do you agree with Madame Lehman?"

The two men replied simultaneously. The older said, "Possibly," and the younger said, "Partially."

George smiled. "A slight difference of opinion—or possibly just shades of an absolute truth. You, sir. You said 'possibly'?"

"Yes." He was a thin, tired, gray man in his late fifties. Well dressed, he looked as if he had had dignity and presence at one time, but that had passed. "I am Paul Barrow. I'm the program chairman of the club. I collect Roman coins."

"Ah, yes. Professor Vandermann mentioned how they were appearing from scuba diving, of all things. Is your link through archaeology too?"

"Only tangentially. I was with the Foreign Service for many years—I retired at the end of my thirty. I was commercial attaché in Paris and then chief of station at the Court of St. James's. I'm an amateur archaeologist of sorts and I came across Vandermann on several digs in England and Normandy."

"Was your knowledge of Roman coins your contribution or did you pick it up at the sites?"

"No, I've been in that field for many years. The coins were my access to the digs. I've specialized in Hadrian and most of the new British sites are turning up from his period."

"Do you think Karl Vandermann was murdered . . . deliberately?

Obviously, he was murdered."

"It's hard to say. Karl was normally an ebullient, optimistic man. Of late he had gotten depressed . . . anxious . . . about something. There was a very apparent change of personality."

The younger man broke in. "He was becoming more like you every day, Paul." He looked directly at George. "Barrow here is the world's prototype of the played-out, despairing, civil servant. He's a classic do-gooder from the Kennedy-Johnson days who thought we could rule the world and cure every ill, and then when he discovered he was wrong he blames it on the decline of American civilization instead of knee-jerk liberalism. We love him, but he'll get you so depressed in thirty minutes you'll want to cut your wrist."

Barrow seemed to take this with more sorrow than resentment. "We're talking about Karl Vandermann, not me, Bob. Karl *was* increasingly concerned—unlike his old self—but I have no idea what was causing it. It could have been university frustrations—having to put up with Charter here would be enough. It may have been personal matters."

"Did he have any conflicts with people here in the club?"

"Not that *I* knew of. He was the father figure to most of us—he created the club, actually welcomed most of the people into it personally."

"Nobody wanted to change directions or were in conflict with the founder?"

"No."

"How about the Executive Committee? How did you all relate to him? Any tensions?"

"I wouldn't think so. He knew I had the greatest admiration for him. He seemed to have a fuller, more satisfying life than anyone I'd ever known. Charter was jealous of him in his department and cutting him from behind whenever he could, but Karl had always dealt with this without stress. He knew Alexa in Germany. She may be able to help you with his life before he came to this country. Who's left? Merton. He'll be along in a minute, but Karl held him in fairly obvious contempt and had for years. And the lovely Eleanor is due too. She took classes under him, but that's the only link I know of there. No, I would be surprised if he was distressed with any of us."

George looked at Charter. "You're Robert Charter? I gather

31

you're at Georgetown with Vandermann." Charter was young, beautifully coiffed, looking like the fashion article just before the foldout.

"Yes, we were in the same department."

"He was a medievalist? What's your specialty?"

"Rise of the Third World countries."

"Really? Kind of the extremes of the time line, isn't that? Are the new countries history yet? I guess they are."

Barrow said, "Vandermann could accept Charter's short and present 'history,' but Charter refused to accept Vandermann's."

Charter snapped back, "Medieval history is storytelling by adults. We have no real idea of what went on back there, and even if we did, what difference does it make? That society was so different from ours there is no application for our times whatsoever. To try to draw analogies is to pile variables on unknowns—you create an absurdity."

George said, "I seem to recall that Vandermann started his career dealing with day-to-day economics in reconstructed Europe. How did he get back to the medieval period?"

There was no sign of recognition on any face except the woman's. "Where did you hear that?" she asked.

George made a gesture of brushing it off. "I don't recall. Dr. Charter . . . it is Doctor, I presume?"

"Yes. Brown. Three years ago."

"You replied 'partially,' did you not? What part do you agree with?"

"I have no reason to think that 'he knew it was coming,' as Madame Lehman would have us believe, nor even that it was long planned. It does seem to me that it was deliberate, though. Not only do all the members of this club collect coins of value, but almost all of us have substantial—in a word, *very* valuable—collections. Almost all of us keep our hoards in safe deposit vaults away from our homes, but it is possible that last night's burglar does not know this, or even that, having stumbled on Vandermann's collection, he will assume that all of ours are sitting on our study desks. I am eager for the burglary to be solved quickly and completely."

"Why *was* the Vandermann collection out of a bank, then?"

"Just incredibly bad luck. He was going to give the program to the club here today—Sunday. His bank would be closed Saturday and Sunday, so he had brought the cabinet home on Friday to

32

prepare for the program. He rarely had more than a half-dozen coins in his house at any one time. Friday he had several hundred."

"Dare I ask how much they would be worth?"

"I don't know his collection that well, but fifty to seventy-five thousand dollars at least, I would suppose."

"More," Barrow said. "Probably twice that."

George whistled with awe, and to Carson's amusement, the missing couple came through the door as if they had been summoned. On further reflection it occurred to him that they might have been standing in the hall, out of sight but listening.

Additional chairs were drawn up to the table, introductions made, and George picked up the conversation quickly to forestall Madame Lehman's setting the scene a second time.

"Miss York . . . ?"

"Eleanor, Mr. George." Eleanor York was in her early thirties, tall, and sun-tanned blonde. She carried herself like a Swedish actress, and struck George as having the most intelligent eyes and full, expressive mouth of anyone he'd ever seen. Carson was more impressed with the perfectly proportioned thighs and a tennis-firmed bottom.

"Eleanor, we've been flirting with a question about Karl Vander-mann's death. Was he killed almost 'accidentally' as an aspect of a burglary in his home or did his death link to his coin collection—or even to this club? Has the idea eve occurred to you?"

Before she could reply, the final member of the group burst in in a thin, reedy voice, "Jesus, no! Who's been giving you that idea? Are the police asking that? If there's anything we don't want it's to have a full-scale police investigation of this club or anybody in it. How did this get started?"

George raised his eyebrows and laughed. "Really? Is there any reason why the club couldn't sustain a police investigation? You're Jerry Merton, was it?" He looked at Merton with distaste, thinking, God help us, he looks like a male librarian is supposed to look: steel-rimmed glasses, colorless, and half-bald. George could remember few live examples of the stereotype, but that didn't keep it from long acceptance.

"No, no. There's nothing underhanded—well, very little. Some of our members are not too careful in reporting profits from their sales at tax time, but the main thing is, we simply don't want it common knowledge that we have coins. The damn things have gotten

33

incredibly valuable, and even if we don't have them at home, there's always the chance of extortion or breaking and entering. We may be one of the few fraternal groups that actually has a reason for secrecy."

"But you advertise your meetings in the papers, don't you? Don't I see coin club meetings in the Sunday edition?"

"Yes, but you notice we never mention names—just places. That's one of the reasons we meet in this public room rather than members' homes."

"Ummm. I'd never thought of that. Incidentally, how common are groups like this? Are there others around Washington?"

"Yes," Merton answered. "There's one or two in each of the suburbs—Chevy Chase, Reston, Montgomery County. There's usually one for people who collect U.S. coins and one for foreign and classic."

"You're the latter?"

"Yes."

"How much contact is there between groups?"

Surprisingly, Merton remained silent and Madame Lehman responded.

"Each club has a recording secretary and they exchange copies of their programs. That way if Annapolis is having a session on Napoleonic gold, for instance, they tell Jerry here and he passes the fact on to me. He knows who's collecting what in our club and tells us when something's happening that we'd be interested in. The specialists can keep track of activities that matter without the knowledge of the people or events becoming public."

George looked at Merton and asked, "You are this club's . . . what did she call it? Recording secretary?"

"Among other things," Merton replied.

"Where do you stand on the question? Do you think Vandermann's death was tied to the people or activities of this club?"

"I do not believe it was in any way. I don't think so myself, and I certainly don't want the authorities to think so—much less the press. Incidentally—nothing personal—but how did *you* get mixed up in this? You should know I was not consulted about your involvement, and I don't see why it's any of your business."

Madame Lehman said, "Karl was talking to Dr. George yesterday about some matters that distressed him concerning the club, and . . ."

34

". . . and you were trying to find out what he knew. As you know, Madame Lehman, ordinarily I have the very highest regard for your judgment on all things, but I disagree with you in this matter totally."

Charter said, "I, on the other hand, have *no* regard for Mr. Merton's judgment on anything—which makes me question my own attitude here, but if it had come from anyone but him, I would agree with his position."

George smothered a grin, and Merton pressed him irritably, "Well, what did Vandermann tell you? What do *you* think you're doing here?"

George laughed out loud. "I'm beginning to wonder myself," he said and ignored the question further. He turned and said, "Miss York . . . Eleanor . . . how do you feel about the matter?"

She was sitting sidewise to the table and responded slowly, first crossing her legs and then pulling her skirt back down by a third of a millimeter. "Dr. Vandermann had suddenly become very worried about something in the past few weeks. We used to have pleasant talks before and after meetings—I'd taken a course from him a few years ago—but these had all disappeared. I couldn't tell what was the matter."

Barrow broke in. "That was true of his relations with all of us, I think. He'd put the club together some ten years ago now, and he used to relish it as a social excuse as much as a numismatic one. That was all gone."

George said, "You know the coins were the least of the silver last night—at least in bulk. Do you think the burglar was really after the coins or was it those trays and coffeepots and things?"

"Oh, the flatware, clearly," Merton reinserted himself. "The coins were an accident. Since silver has gone sky-high the metal is the fastest way to make more money with less risk than anything you can steal."

"Can it be sold?"

"Easily. There's always been a good, legitimate market for buying and selling household silver. It's essentially untraceable."

"But you said coins had become very valuable too. And they're easier to transport—small and unbreakable . . ."

"Quite different. You don't understand . . ."

George swept the group with his eyes. "Mr. Merton here says the thief was after the . . . what did you call it? Flatware? Do you

35

agree?"

The Executive Committee nodded except for Madame Lehman, who was watching the group closely.

"Mr. Merton," George asked, "what do you do for a living?"

"I'm chief accountant at Thomas Jefferson University Hospital, and I think it's time for our turn, sir. Could we ask *you* some questions?"

"No," George replied without changing tone or cadence, "I'm sorry to say I'm afraid the time I have available has run out, and before we get involved in any general discussion, I need some data to work from. Madame Lehman, if you'll excuse us, I'd like to abandon you now with the promise that I will call you shortly after noon tomorrow with my thoughts on the matter. Would you forgive us if we moved on to another appointment?"

To Carson's astonishment, she burst into a throaty laugh and said, "I think that is precisely what you should do. I can give you my phone number, and if you need to ask me anything, do not hesitate to call."

"I will be pleased to do that."

"Can I walk with you to the stairs?"

"We would be honored."

They all scrambled to their feet and made their departure. As soon as they were alone in the hall, George asked, "Madame Lehman, what was that charade all about? Rather than there being a vast consensus, you seem to be the only member of that group that believes Vandermann's death links to the club, and there's no great agreement that he knew it was coming."

"You're quite right, of course. Mostly I wanted to see what they would say before an outsider—and I did want to see if Karl had spoken to anyone but you and me. From what they said, I would think not. What do you think?"

"I haven't decided what I think yet. One of my choices is that you know a great deal about the matter and were trying to find out how much everyone else knows—which is to say, you wished to know if anyone suspected you of being involved. Your charm and your beauty have forced me to abandon this suspicion, of course."

She laughed again. "Oh, I do hope so. Call me when you've made up your mind. I will not plead for your help. I believe that your personal sense of integrity will bring you to our side."

" 'Our side?' I couldn't tell so clearly who was with you . . . 'us'

. . . and who wasn't."

She smiled and said, "I think your young friends here would say, 'Think about it.' You'll see. Thank you so much for coming."

Not until they were alone on the sidewalk again did Carson say, "And what game were *you* playing up there? You failed to ask every question I thought you were going to and kept beating on ones you either knew the answer to already or didn't really care about."

George appeared to be enjoying himself immensely. "Thank you. Observant as always. Crighton, are the Info Bank and Capital Line up on Sundays?"

"I think so."

"Good. We go then to the computer."

5

BUT THERE WAS A SHORT DELAY.

The Audi had been parked a few spaces down the block. They had walked to it, gotten in, and Crighton was backing to pull away from the curb when Eleanor York burst out of the Tavern and looked anxiously up and down the sidewalk.

"Wait a minute," Carson said to Crighton and rolled down his window. He stuck his head out and shouted, "Can we help?"

The girl looked relieved and hurried toward them. "Is there a chance you're going back to Washington? I badly need a ride."

"Sure, where are you headed? Climb in."

"Just get me near a Metro stop. I can take it from there."

She slid into the back seat beside George, and Crighton moved out into traffic.

"You haven't got car trouble, have you?" George asked. "Did you drive or did you come with Mr. Merton?"

38

"No, Merton brought me, but I don't have the strength to defend myself all the way home. Comrade Merton is much more active than he looks."

Crighton grinned and Carson looked concerned.

"What role does Merton play in that club?" George asked.

"Mainly he's the secretary-treasurer and he is a strange little shrimp. I've never understood why Dr. Vandermann relied on him so. I think he's held the job ever since Karl founded the club. He putters around and keeps the books and sends out announcements and makes the convention arrangements and generally fades into the plaster—at least everybody thinks he does. In fact, he pounds my ear continually about how nobody appreciates him. He can talk and use his hands at the same time."

"I gather you get more than your share of his attention."

"Ha!" She laughed in good humor. "At least I appeal to him more than the men in the group. I think he considers us fellow professionals—both in the same business. Health, of course."

"Health?"

"Didn't you know? I'm a nurse . . . dental."

"Amazing," George said. " 'The dental assistant.' There was bound to be some of you somewhere, but I've never seen one just walking around loose. Isn't that odd? We visit you people twice a year—yet I've never seen one of you out of captivity before."

They laughed together, and Eleanor said, "I suspect we pass ourselves off as something else whenever we can."

Carson asked, "Are you the kind that stuffs all those things into the mouth, or the 'we haven't been using our floss, have we?' type?"

"Neither. I'm the 'once we get it in place you won't be able to tell it from your own' kind. I did the others on the way up, though, so I know all the lines."

"Dental assistants have the sexiest legs of any women in the world," said Carson. "You must have a course on when to lean across the patient's arm. I have a dentist named Grieg who has his girls so well trained that just as he goes down for the kill, they lean over in the most suggestive way. It's as if they've run their hands up the back of your neck . . . I'd never thought of it before, but that takes real skill. Caressed by the fronts of two thighs." He seemed to be running his memory back through treasured fillings, exciting extractions, remembered incidents recaptured with pleasure.

39

Crighton jerked the steering wheel deliberately and then said sweetly, "Strange, I don't seem to remember any of that ever happening to me. Am I missing something? Delights denied?"

The women shared a look and a laugh, and Eleanor said, "I have no idea what you're talking about, Mr. Carson."

"Steve."

"Steve."

George frowned for a moment and then said, "Eleanor, how much of a hurry are you in? You might be of great help, if you could spare us an hour."

"I'd love to. I do have a supper date, but it's not till seven and the afternoon is still young."

"Yes. If what I have in mind works, you might find it interesting, and I could use your vocabulary. I want to establish what is *not* true in our present dilemma, so we can concentrate on what is. I'll explain as soon as we get to the library. Crighton, how are we doing?"

"Ten minutes, Mr. George."

"Charge ahead," he said.

And in ten minutes they were there. By twenty they were in a glass-enclosed booth in the Reference Department of the Werner-Bok Library. Six printer terminals were lined down either wall, but none was in use, and they had the room to themselves. En route through the Reference Room they had acquired a singularly angelic-looking reference librarian, and George thought, Thank God there are librarians to be; this young lady could only be a librarian or a nun. She had huge, China-blue eyes and combed her hair straight down from a dead-center part. She pointed out folding chairs and snapped on a terminal.

"Miss Arnette, we're not quite as helpless as your off-the-street visitors, but we could use a little assistance with your toy there. Could you get us started, please?"

It was clear the toy label pained the lady, but she was too polite to say so. Instead she asked, "Have you ever used a CRT in a reference mode?"

"Yes. We have them at Yale, but I think we want Capital Line here. I've trained on Info Bank and Lockheed. Are the protocols similar?"

"Very close." Miss Arnette juggled some display cards and ended with a set that she placed on a miniature easel beside the cathode ray tube. "There are your questions. The commands can be either four-letter acronyms or single-letter codes. Capitol Line is both key word in context and thesaurus."

"Excellent. If you'll bring it up, I'd like to start with thesaurus terms."

Miss Arnette seated herself in front of the terminal and the four visitors pulled chairs around her, with George peering over her right arm.

"Let me explain a bit what we're doing here," he said to his audience. "I presume you've all used a computer terminal as a bibliographic device—a glorified card catalog?"

Carson nodded, but the women shook their heads.

"Well, in that form, the librarians have simply typed copies of their catalog cards into the computer, the computer has stored the copies, and you can get them back by asking for them by the traditional author, title, or subject. As far as use goes, the chief advantage is your ability to limit—'show me *only* books in English' or '*only* books published in the last two years.' But here, we're going to play games with it in the reference mode—not the bibliographic. With the invention of the New York Times Info Bank back in the early seventies, they started putting *text* in the machines not just titles. You could get the answer—the actual information you wanted—right off the TV tube, not just a list of books or articles to go to to read about it. Info Bank is national and New York. Capital Line is based on Washington-area papers. What's actually in it, Miss Arnette?"

"The Washington *Post* and the *Star,* and the Alexandria *Gazette,* and eight regional papers like the Montgomery County *News,* Fairfax . . ."

"Good. That's enough. Let's start our questions in big loops. What do you find on Robberies?"

Miss Arnette typed "GVME ROBBERY," which appeared on the screen. The computer typed its own line below it: "CAPITAL LINE FINDS 2101."

"Is that a code number?" Carson asked.

"No," George replied, "I suspect that it is saying, 'I find 2,101 different news stories that have been given the subject heading 'Robbery.' "

Miss Arnette nodded. "That is correct."

"Those are whole stories, not just the number of times it found the word 'robbery'?"

"That's right."

"Do we need to add synonyms for 'Robbery'?"

"I doubt it. Let's see." She typed in "DSPL ROBBERY." "I've asked it to display what all 'Robbery' includes."

The computer typed out on its screen, "THE TERM ROBBERY INCLUDES ROBBERIES, BURGLARY, BURGLARIES, LARCENY, THEFT, THEFTS. DO YOU WISH TO LIMIT THE TERM?"

"Do you?" Miss Arnette asked.

"No, leave it broad, but let's limit time," George said. "How many hits do you get if you . . . Eleanor, your friend Merton says this was just a silverware robbery—and Steve, the police say they've been getting a lot of silver jobs. How long has this been going on, would you say?"

Carson said, "It sounded like they were talking about a year or so."

"Two years should do it," Eleanor agreed.

Without waiting, Miss Arnette typed in the limiting years. The computer quickly read, "CAPITAL LINE FINDS 911."

"Better," said George. "But still much too large. All right, let's cut to silver. Miss Arnette, just give us robberies involving silver in the past two years."

Miss Arnette typed and the computer replied, "CAPITAL LINE FINDS NONE."

"What does that mean?" George asked.

"I suspect it means that the program does not analyze robberies by what is taken. Let me try something." She typed, "GVME SILVER."

The computer replied, "CAPITAL LINE FINDS 105."

"That's what I thought. Those will be articles about silver as an economic term. 'The price of silver fell in Switzerland.' We're going to have to go to key word in context."

As she typed instructions and the computer screen cleared, responded, and cleared again, George explained, "Now we'll be searching the articles themselves, not the subject headings the librarians gave them. There's a use for both approaches. You don't use the names of race horses or characters in TV shows as subject headings, but you may want to search on them. On the other hand, if you're looking for laws that affect juvenile delinquents, it's useless to look for those words in the statutes. Laws say 'below the age of twenty-one' or 'aged eighteen or younger,' not 'juvenile delinquents who steal cars.' You need 'juvenile delinquents' assigned as a subject heading to pull them all together. Here we're in trouble since there is no subject heading called 'silver robberies.' "

Without waiting, Miss Arnette had commanded a different program and had typed, "GVME SILVER AND ROBBERY OR ROBBERIES OR THEFT OR LARCENY OR BREAK-IN," and she had limited it to the past two years.

"Now she's using what's called Boolean logic—the use of ands and ors to link or reject. The computer will be searching its memory for these precise words. Miss Arnette, does Capital Line use abstracts or original text?"

"Original text. The first three paragraphs or the first fifty lines of type in the news story, whichever is longer."

The computer said, "CAPITAL LINE FINDS 65."

"Now we're talking. Now let's see how these silver robberies fall by area. Miss Arnette, start with Fairfax County, and you folks help me with the others. I know Alexandria and the District. What else do we have in the so-called metropolitan area?"

Working quickly they discovered that the thefts were distributed surprisingly uniformly around the Washington scene. The only difference appeared related to the size of the governmental units, not the frequency of the thefts.

"Jesus," Carson said. "They really are common, aren't they? Fairfax County had over thirty in two years? No wonder they flipped ours off so casually."

George appeared bemused. "Yes, this is frustrating. Not only does this make it quite possible that the Vandermann break-in was only part of a common occurrence, but the distribution throughout the area is so general there appear to be no special targets. For our purposes, I'm not sure whether it's good or bad."

"Wait a minute," Crighton said. "Let's get at it from the other side. How many break-ins involved coins?"

"Good," said George. "Eleanor, should we be using any other words?"

"Maybe crowns or numismatics, but coins are what the papers usually call them."

"Fine. Miss Arnette, can you run that for us?"

43

She stroked in the proper terms and the limiters and the computer replied, "CAPITAL LINE FINDS 16."

"Hmmm," said George. "Sixteen coin burglaries. Very interesting. Let's see how those distribute."

Carson used the hits of the "silver robbery" sheet as a tally list and noted the numbers found under "coins" beside them. At the conclusion of this exercise, Carson said, "I don't know what it means, but we have an aberration this time. Look: Montgomery County six, the District six, Prince Georges two, and Columbia two. None in Virginia at all. Just D.C. and Maryland."

Eleanor suddenly leaned forward, getting into the spirit of the game. "Can you try *silver* coins now?"

Miss Arnette did and the computer replied, "CAPITAL LINE FINDS 16."

"How about gold coins?"

"CAPITAL LINE FINDS NONE."

"Try U.S. or American or United States."

"CAPITAL LINE FINDS NONE."

"Try English coins."

The computer replied, "CAPITAL LINE FINDS 16."

"Bingo," Carson said quietly.

Eleanor frowned and suddenly moved closer to the terminal, her fingers running across her lips reflectively. The group remained silent, letting the girl develop her thought without interruption. She asked slowly, "Can you try those sixteen by day?"

The librarian quickly made seven passes, at the end of which she said, "They all fell on Saturdays or Sundays."

"Umm." Another pause and then, "Does the word 'arrested' or 'suspect' appear in any of the stories?"

The terms were tested and the computer replied, "CAPITAL LINE FINDS NONE."

"Wow," she said softly. "Apparently not a single person has been caught. Ummm . . . ask it if the word handcuffs or handcuffed appears in any of the sixteen."

"CAPITAL LINE FINDS 16," the computer replied.

"Jesus," Carson said under his breath. "Every one!"

"Does it find the word killed or dead . . . or death?" Eleanor asked almost inaudibly.

"CAPITAL LINE FINDS 3," the computer said.

"Where?"

Miss Arnette stroked and then summarized what they all could see, "One in Montgomery County, one in Prince Georges, and one in the District."

"Jesus H . . ." Carson exploded. "Wait a minute. Why isn't Vandermann showing up?"

Miss Arnette replied, "When did it happen? The data base sometimes takes a day or so to update."

"No," Eleanor said. "It's probably because we're looking under coins and silver and theft. There was no theft, so silver would not be mentioned, and certainly the coins didn't make the papers. Nothing happened to the coins at all."

"That's right," George said. "Eleanor, that was very well done. You've found our targets. Miss Arnette, we're ready to read those sixteen articles. Can you bring them up, please? Full text."

She stroked in the proper instructions and the computer streamed a paragraph across the center of the screen.

"Shit!" said the virginal Miss Arnette.

"What?" Carson burst out laughing.

" 'The Capital Line program will be inoperative for approximately four hours for system maintenance and update,' " she read. The message was frozen on the screen and the service was quite dead.

6

DAMMIT, THAT WAS FRUSTRATING," CARSON said.

It was now four o'clock, with the Werner-Bok closing at five on Sundays. Crighton had gone off with Eleanor to return her to her Arlington apartment, and the two men were seating themselves in Crighton's office in the Werner-Bok's basement.

"Maddening," Carson added.

George sighed. "It could be worse. At least we know there's something there. Does that sort of thing happen often when you use the terminals?"

"Often, hell! Invariably. At least it told us *why* it was going down. Usually it freezes halfway between a question and an answer and there you sit staring at the last message not knowing whether it's down for a thirty-second hiccup or the rest of the week. You sit there playing insoluble games with yourself asking now what is logical here? I've waited five minutes. Should I wait just a few

46

minutes more since surely it's about to come up, or do I conclude that if it was only a minor problem it would have responded already and therefore it's something massive and will be dead for hours? Then again . . . It is infuriating."

"Are you describing your computer research just at the Werner-Bok or at all the libraries you've used?"

"Oh, no. This constant up-and-down, on-and-dead business is universal. I never met a library where it wasn't like that. Just exasperating. The curse is that when they do work they are so damn good that you waste precious time hoping they'll come up again because when they are working they are enormously efficient—cut hours off your research time and lead you into places you'd never have thought of with the old tools."

"Well, we've still got an hour before this place closes, so let's lean on the old tools for now."

"Really? Is there anything to be done? I thought your two-day deadline had had it. You keeping up the good fight?"

"Oh, surely," George said with cheerful relish. "We're doing fine. We're discarding dead wood right on schedule. One more hour. Just time for you to make certain there's nothing we should know from city directories. I'll try a tête-à-ear with Madame Lehman."

"City directories? Come on . . . wha-a-t?"

"There may be nothing there, but let's be sure before we write them off. There's no reason they can't serve as the poor man's Who's Who for common folk. Do you remember what's in a city directory?"

"Street numbers, I assume."

"That's only one part. The main section is an alphabetical listing that gives addresses and phone numbers and the like, but it also gives the individual's occupation, the name of his employer, who else lives at the address, marital status—divorced, widowed, and such."

"Who are we using this on?"

"Let's start with our friends in the Executive Committee."

"Don't we already know everything about them that we could get from a city directory?"

"Probably. I simply want to be able to say with certainty: 'There's nothing useful there. Forget it.' I'd hate to find that Karl Vandermann is carried as 'also known as Joseph Goebbels, moved into present address 1945, previous employer German government.' "

"You're kidding, of course."

47

"Of course."

Carson sighed and rose to his feet. "Where do I get one of these things?"

"Why don't you take yourself back up to the angelic Miss Arnette. See if she'll let you go on deck and work with the full set."

"Wait a minute. Am I supposed to be working backward—looking for discontinuities, did you call them? Like the Who's Who bit?"

"That's the idea."

"Well, that makes a little more sense. Sorry. Forgive me for doubting you. I'll be back by closing time," he said and disappeared around the doorjamb.

George settled himself comfortably into Crighton's office chair and rolled it closer to her desk. The satisfied smile on his face seemed to be a mixture of contentment with the way his puzzle was proceeding and anticipation of the coming conversation. He extracted his note case from an inside coat pocket, found the number Alexa Lehman had given him, and dialed.

She answered, and George said, "Hello there, Edward George here. Thanks for being home."

"I promised you I would be. How can I help?"

"Well, I'm doing as I promised too, and I'm gathering data. If I do say so, I've done every bit as well as I'd hoped and better than I expected! Raw data Number 206: I really should know where everyone was last night."

"Logical," she said.

"You recall we probably saw the killer ourselves—right in front of us. I have to say probably because Karl Vandermann may have been dead even before we arrived, but we were told last night it would have been only minutes before. I presume you know where everyone was at eight o'clock last evening?"

She laughed. "With your suspicious mind, if I answer yes you'll think I was establishing an alibi for myself."

"True," he said cheerfully, "but with your lively mind, I suspect you would do it just to be on the safe side, involved or not. So candor won't do you much more damage than discretion would."

She laughed again and said, "Very well. Got a pencil or how's your memory? Karl Vandermann was in his home, of course. Robert Charter was with a female graduate student 'at her place,' I believe is the way it's expressed. Jerry Merton had spent the day looking at the fall colors on the Skyline Drive and was driving home—alone.

Paul Barrow went to an old movie at a theatre near the Thomas Jefferson campus—also alone. I asked Eleanor York over to my apartment and we had supper together here and looked at television tapes of some old *I, Claudius* episodes. And . . . I believe that's everybody," she said.

"Ummm, you did indeed know where everyone was. I'm not even going to guess why you'd gone to all that trouble—though I was sure you would have. How do you like the reports yourself? Believe them all?"

"Well, let's see. If the graduate student was dependent on Robert Charter's approval of her thesis, I'm sure she would be happy to say they were together whether they were or not. In my day we would give up something more difficult to replace than a spoken paragraph for something as valuable as that.

"Mr. Merton could have come home any time from breakfast on and still claim he was on the Drive—even report some phenomena he'd seen to give it credence. Paul admits himself he'd seen the picture a dozen times so he hardly needed to see it again to tell us what was in it. No, the reports are all useless if one of them really was at Karl's house last night."

"You didn't evaluate your own. Do you and Miss York frequently have supper and spend an evening together?"

"Well done. She had never been in my house before—indeed I have never seen her more than a block away from Gadsby's until last night. I think I terrify her—and her values are a great deal different from mine."

"So, if you were wishing to e✦ablish a firm alibi for yourself, this would be the most dramatic way you could come up with one."

"Oh, my no. Not the most dramatic—just the easiest to control. Requiring the least effort."

"What a delight you are, Madame, but how fatiguing it would be to try to get ahead of you."

"You don't have to get ahead. But just keeping abreast might be fun, don't you think?"

"I do indeed. As the diarists used to say, 'Of which more anon.' Now I must concentrate on our problem. I do hope you are more of a distraction from it than a part of it."

"Oh, so do I, Dr. George," she said, "so do I," and they parted.

Edward George smiled and shook his head. Interesting woman, he thought, and probably very dangerous. Indeed, weren't they all.

49

The only difference was *how* they were dangerous. What nonsense the Movement's insistence that they were really just like men. Nothing in seventy years' experience bore that out. Ah well, he sighed. Back at it.

He flipped backward in his note case that still lay on the desk and dialed another number.

"Fairfax County Police Department," it answered.

"I'd like to talk to somebody who's working on that Vandermann murder case, please. Lieutenant Price will do if he's there. If not, anybody who knows about it."

Price was there and he came on. "Hi!" George continued cheerfully. "This is Edward George. We talked last night. You recall I was one of the two men who found the Vandermann body." Price remembered but without enthusiasm. "I was just wondering if anything new had developed?"

"No," Price said rather curtly. "Have you remembered something we should know?"

"No. Are you still convinced it was another one of your silver robberies?"

"It would have been if you hadn't scared him off. Or something did."

"Was anyone killed in any of the others?"

"No."

"How about setting the victim in a chair and handcuffing his hands behind him?"

"That was new."

"Somebody told me that there had been thirty or forty silver burglaries in Fairfax County in the past two years. Is that true?"

"I have no idea. I don't think I ever counted them. Who told you that?"

"I can't recall. Must have been someone at the courthouse last night. Do you folks compare notes with your neighboring jurisdictions?"

"We circulate Xeroxes describing certain kinds of crimes and we try to keep track of this sort of thing."

"There's no central place to compare crimes or operating techniques for the Washington area?"

"Lord, no." Lieutenant Price was having difficulty retaining his civility. With some effort he spelled out, "Mr. . . . uh, George. Do you realize that there are nearly three million people spread out in thirty-five different jurisdictions straddling three states here? Last year we had over seven *thousand* armed robberies in the Washington area—with sixty people killed in the process. We trade information on some murders and all bank jobs, and that's about it. That's about all we can handle. If we distribute more data, the 'noise' would be so great we couldn't spot anything important."

"Isn't there a computer center for the area?"

"No. Back in the early seventies, most jurisdictions put in some kind of automation with LEAA funds, but it was for their own units. The only ones that overlap boundaries are the car license bureaus. We all have access to each other's automobile records."

"Ummm. Have you solved any of the silver break-ins yet?"

"Of course. We cleared ten or fifteen of 'em with the arrest of a bunch of teen-agers last summer, and . . . no, I guess the other was an antique gun series. But we'll close this thing down one of these days. This is the kind of crime that when you do break it, you clear a whole bunch of cases at the same time."

"What about the metallic purple car we saw. Have you been able to trace it?"

"It would have helped if you'd got the license . . ."

"Sorry. We're not used to reacting that way when something unusual happens. I've been trying to reconstruct it in my mind, but I wonder if the license wasn't obscured in some way. I can't even see where it would fit on the car. But there was no question of the color or of those tongues of flames painted around the sides. Surely there can't be too many like that even among thirty-five jurisdictions! Isn't that pretty important?"

"Isn't what pretty important?"

"The purple car," George said patiently. "Superficially, at least, it would seem that someone running out of a house where a body was soon to be found and jumping into a purple car to drive away at high speed might attract your attention . . ."

"Oh, we put out an APB. Purple cars run pretty heavily to the Hispanic sections of the District."

"You recalled the flames painted on the sides?"

"Yeah, but that's not much help."

"Oh? Why not?"

"Those flame things are like stick-on labels. They come on sheets of wax paper and they peel 'em off the paper and stick 'em on the car by hand."

51

"But they're still pretty unusual, aren't they? Won't they be easy for the police to spot?"

"They'll be long gone by now—hardly worth looking for. They can be peeled off just about as easy as you can stick 'em on. By now that guy's pretty sure to have stripped his off and put 'em in the trash. I don't suppose you have any further thoughts about the bird you saw run out of the house? Have you decided what he yelled yet? You still think it was Spanish?"

"Ummm. Mr. Carson and I have discussed that but we can't add much to what we told you. The figure was essentially small, but in that outfit you couldn't tell much about size. At least it wasn't sufficiently tall to stand out—or up. The voice was high—either a man using falsetto or a woman shrieking. Last night I thought it said 'Escaparate' and I thought it would turn out to be a cognate of 'escape,' but I looked it up and that word means 'shop window.' Something wrong there. I wonder if there's such a word in Italian or Arabic?"

"I wouldn't have any idea," Price said.

"Me either. Lieutenant, I sense you're not overly sanguine about solving this case any time soon."

"Look, Mr. . . . George." Price had reached the more-in-sorrow-than-in-anger point. "You're like everybody who's had their first crime. It's the biggest thing that's ever happened to you. You expect everybody to drop everything and run around working on *your* file. We get hundreds of crimes all the time. There are only so many of us and we pick our shots and we pace ourselves. The easy ones we do first. The harder ones next—the ones we have some chance of breaking. Yours fits in with a whole bunch of these things. We're chipping away on 'em and one day they'll crack and we'll solve a whole drawerful. We're working on it. We'll get it done. Just remember, though, that you're just one of lots. Okay?"

George smiled to himself. He was not perturbed mainly because he was not surprised. He had met this attitude before, and he had always wondered if he'd been stuck with thirty years of endless antisocial acts if he wouldn't have become pretty glazed himself. But his conscience was now clear. He'd given "the authorities" every chance and he was now convinced if this was going to be solved soon—indeed maybe ever—he was going to have to do it himself. He now owed them only civil courtesy.

52

"Yes indeed, Lieutenant. I do appreciate the time you've given me and your patience. If there's anything I can do to help, I hope you won't fail to call. I've enjoyed talking with you."

George chuckled as he returned the phone to its cradle. They can't say we haven't been cooperative. Oh, really? he thought. How's your wife? Compared to what? He grinned grimly and turned to a blank page in his note case. He stared at this for a moment, pursed his lips, and began to write.

At that moment Crighton was sitting with Eleanor York in front of the latter's Virginia high rise, with the Audi's motor running.

"This coin scene seems a bit odd for you. How deeply are you into it?" Crighton asked.

"Would you believe, I've been at it for years. I sort of backed into it at the beginning, but it has its moments. It put me through school, among other things."

Crighton shook her head. "What's the motivation for the group as a whole? Is it to make money or is it the historical bit that Dr. Vandermann was giving us when we first met him?"

"Yes," Eleanor said and laughed. "Yes. It's both—it's the whole thing. There must be forty or fifty people in that club and they run from one end of the reasons to the other. There are guys who follow the auction charts like the stock market and 'reevaluate' the worth of their collections every week. Sometimes every day! There are the Julius-Caesar-touched-this-very-coin types who have to cross their legs and breathe hard when they see an Etruscan bottle top. Strange. Some of the weirdest specimens are the one-coin people or the provenance types.

"The provenance people don't care what the coin is, just who owned it. They'll hold up a Robert the Bruce penny and say, 'This originally belonged to the Duke of Carlisle who sold it to the Warden at the Bodleian who willed it to the Vicar of Wakefield, who . . .'" She waved her hands.

"And the one coin?"

"The one-coiners collect just one solitary kind of coin, but try to get every known version of it. They have it by dates and by mints and by off-centers and by use and by weight—and who knows what. I'm in the early English thing, you know, and in my series the one-coiners really freak you out. You take a Henry III penny—he struck

53

them over a fifty-year period, he struck them in over forty different castles—the castle name is on the back along with the name of the man who made the coin and there are over three hundred of these moneyers. Some guys have spent their whole lives just chasing down combinations of one moneyer on this one variety of coin. They follow some old Saxon from one castle to another for fifty years—beyond belief!"

"Are there that many of the coins left around? When was—who did you say?—Henry III?"

"Oh, he ran from 1216 to 1272, but he had two things going for him that were different from most. Most of the kings either didn't live long enough to make too many coins—someone as famous as Henry V or Richard the Lionhearted were only in office a few years—or the guy that followed them called in all the coins and had them melted down and reissued with his own name on them. That way, about all we have of theirs is what got buried in wartime or had rolled down a crack. But Henry III was in for half a century, he fought wars all over France, and he struck coins by the thousands to pay off the soldiers. When he went home, his coins stayed in France where they'd been used to buy provisions, and they had so much more silver in them than anything the French had that the French kept using them for generations! The ensuing French kings made no attempt to melt them down, so they're quite common now."

"Comparatively speaking."

Eleanor laughed. "Comparatively."

"How much would one of them be worth?"

"Well, that's when you get into the other end of the spectrum—making money off money. When I bought my first Henry III pennies—and it's only been ten or twelve years ago—they cost about ten dollars apiece. Now those same coins are worth eighty to a hundred just lying there in the bank drawer. These coins have gone up at well over twenty percent per year, which is a good deal better than bonds—even better than real estate. They're easy to cash back to money too—and you don't have to trade in a whole house just to get a few dollars."

"And you're in it for the money? How come you know so much about moneyers and how long the kings reigned? Are you sure there isn't just a hair of romance in their appeal to you too?"

"Very little. You have to know those kinds of things to know which ones are rare—which ones to pay what for. A William the

54

Conqueror penny struck at Salisbury is going for a hundred dollars these days. The same penny struck at Hastings sold for over five hundred last week."

"Scarcer?"

"Scarcer."

"Sold to who?"

"Good question. That's the real story of antique collecting today. When I got started as a freshman at Georgetown, my kind of coins were being bought almost exclusively by kids and granddads. It was a hobby. Then in 1970 everybody went off the silver standard. Remember when we quit making silver dimes and quarters and started these greasy sandwich things with copper centers? The British did the same thing, and suddenly all the doctors and bankers began to buy old coins to ride the inflation wagon up. Now, bless their hearts, the Arabs are using 'em to put money away for their old age or something, and the prices have gone into orbit. Madame Lehman was a rich woman with the gold collection she brought with her from Europe. Thanks to our Arab friends, she may well be a millionaire before very long—if she isn't already."

"You're kidding. She's intimidating enough without real money behind her."

" 'Intimidating.' Beautiful. That is precisely the word. She certainly is that very thing."

"I've got to go," Crighton said, thinking that the Arabs were going to get rich on her idling car if this kept up, "but I can't help asking about your friend Merton. I can't believe he's got you on the defensive."

Eleanor laughed cheerfully. "That creep. He is a strange little man. Karl couldn't stand him and Paul Barrow leaves the room if he comes in. He's always trying to con Bob Charter and the Madame, so I guess I'm the only one he's got to talk to—even if I didn't wear a skirt."

"Con them on what?"

"He's always wanted to start a small time health insurance operation, and he tried to beg some seed money from Charter for most of last year. Every now and then when he gets his nerve up, he tries to get some of the Lehman's cash, but neither one of them has come across yet. They're rather gentle with him when they say no, and I haven't quite figured that out. As a rule, neither of them is very subtle when they're turned off with somebody."

55

"This is fascinating. The more you talk the less likely it all sounds! Do you suppose we could have lunch someday . . ."

"I'd love to. Want to pick a time and I'll go up and check my calendar . . ."

"Why don't you call me? I'm at the library, of course, and I suspect you have a lot livelier life than I do!"

They laughed together, and Eleanor said, "Oh, I don't know. With your looks and your figure, if it's so you've got no one to blame but yourself."

She winked and they said their good-byes as she headed toward the gold and glass lobby.

Five minutes later Crighton was looping up onto Memorial Bridge, and it was at precisely that moment that Edward George looked up from his notes and said to himself, That's it. I know who killed Karl Vandermann.

7

By THE TIME CRIGHTON REACHED THE Werner-Bok they were closing the doors for the night. Guards had driven George and Carson before them and they had been extruded, along with a dozen glazed scholars, out the Mall entrance. The guards pulled the great bronze doors shut behind them, whereupon Crighton arrived at the foot of the steps.

"Perfect timing," said George, as he and Carson slid into the car. "That is real efficiency. Steve just arrived and we'd barely gotten through the door when you showed up. It's council-of-war time. Where should we go?"

"Let me say at once," said Carson, "that that fool idea of yours to look in city directories was very successful. I just may have flushed out something. Wherever we go it should have large tables and bright lights. I want to spread some paper around."

"Why not the National Gallery?" Crighton asked.

"They have food?" said George.

"Oh, they put in a beautiful dining room under that waterfall between the two buildings. You haven't seen it? Very classy. They have this modern fountain up here on street level, and then the water falls down a slope into the basement and you eat beside it below ground. Much splashing and movement . . ."

". . . and a slight sense of vertigo," said Carson. "But the food's good."

They agreed and Crighton circled the library and gallery, parking in front of the museum on the Mall side. With great reluctance George resisted the paintings and they went directly to the cellar restaurant.

During the meal, Crighton gave the men a detailed report of her conversation with Eleanor York, while George continued to nod and say, "Yes," "Good," and "It all fits."

When she had finished, Crighton said, "What's with all this affirmation? Did you know all that already?"

"No, no. It was all new and fascinating. Very valuable. While you two were gathering data, I tried to sort out what we'd learned so far and I've got a theory. My agreement only meant just what I said: everything you found out from the lady fit into my . . . hypothesis?"

"Come on," Carson said, "let's hear it. What have you got?"

"No, let me be sure you didn't find something that washes it down the drain. What was in the city directories?"

"Very interesting," Carson said eagerly. He pulled a sheaf of crumpled call slips from his pockets and began to place them on the cleared tabletop.

"To begin with, you failed to warn me that there would be a whole mess of different volumes to plow through. It turns out that there is a different city directory for D.C., one for Alexandria, one for Arlington, one for Chevy Chase and Bethesda, et cetera, et cetera. But I faithfully tried 'em all for the past twenty years."

"How many names did you track?"

"Six. Of course they were all there to start with, but as I worked backward they began to drop off. The tricky part was Barrow. He kept coming and going. Three years abroad, then three years here, then three years abroad, and so on."

George smiled and said, "Good experience for you. It'll strengthen your character."

"My character is . . . never mind. Okay. Here we go. Jones, you'll have to tell me what these addresses mean. I don't know the area well enough to generalize the districts yet."

He dealt six piles, each with the name of one of the Executive Committee on it, and then hastily arranged each pile by descending date.

"I apologize for the paper. In candor, I had so little confidence in your goose chase that I didn't take anything with me to write on. As you can see, I ended up digging dead call slips out of wastebaskets. To work . . .

"Brother Vandermann has been here since the fifties. Throughout, his employer was Georgetown University, and you can see through the years he has been listed as instructor, assistant professor, associate professor, assistant chairman. Everything in proper order. The only thing that appears to be news is his addresses. He's only lived in three houses. Crite, do these tell us anything?"

She picked up the three and said, "Wardman Park Residence Hotel, Congressional Towers, and Fairfax on the Parkway. All very well-heeled spots. He started at a level most people end at."

"Right," said Carson. "I suspected so.

"Charter," he continued. "Only been here three years. Instructor, then assistant professor *immediately*. Apparent status with a brand-new Ph.D. Moved up too fast. Why? Did he know someone or did he have something on somebody? Just one address from the beginning: The Watergate Hotel."

"Very large money," said Crighton. "Never do it on a teaching salary."

"That's what I thought.

"Madame Lehman. Been here the longest. Always lived alone. Lived at a street address—3060 R Street—until just a couple of years ago."

"That's Georgetown, across from Dumbarton Oaks. If she owned the whole house it cost at least two hundred thousand dollars. Probably more."

"Uh-huh. Then two years ago she moved to the Legate Towers."

"Also big money. The apartments cover whole floors, with wood-burning fireplaces on all levels."

"You see the pattern. There's lots of money floating around that bunch. Now we get to the proletariat. Paul Barrow. Like I said, he

59

came and went. Obviously the rotating foreign service officer bit. Every loop he comes up one. 'Officer in Foreign Assistance Division,' 'Assistant Director Commodity Aid Bureau,' 'Director Foreign Policy Advisory Staff,' and so on. Every time he comes back he lives at a different place. Here, do they tell you anything, Crite?"

She leafed through them and said, "Nothing special. He stayed in the suburbs. Most of the ones I recognize are near bus lines, and a lot of 'em are garden apartment complexes. Routine government worker, it would appear."

"Right. If he was making money, he didn't plow it into housing. Not so your friend, E. York. Look. While she was at Georgetown, she's listed at addresses always with four or six people. Rooming houses? Shared apartments?"

"Could be. They're all near the campus."

"Note they're all women. Disappointingly straight."

"In your ear, Carson."

"But the moment she leaves school, she goes to a single address. Does it signify anything?"

"Yes, one of those black glass luxury jobs overlooking the Potomac."

"Then that one . . ."

"That's her present condo. Very classy."

"On a dental assistant's salary?"

"She admitted herself she had a good thing going with those coins."

"Either that or Daddy is well heeled—whoever Daddy may be."

"I'll explore that when I see her."

"But I build to my big finish. Your attention is called to the largest pile of all. The peripatetic Mr. Merton. Are you ready? Reading chronologically, I give you his occupational progression: Arnie's Used Cars, The Anti-vivisection League, Florida Paradise Estates, Golden Years City, Allied Industrial Health Insurance, Thomas Jefferson University Hospital."

They laughed and Crighton asked, "How many years did all that take?"

"Twelve. He was averaging two years a stop."

"No," said George. "At the time the directory company was making its annual survey, he gave the appearance of two years per stop. You may be short an aluminum siding franchise and a vacuum cleaner route simply because they were out of phase."

60

"You've got the picture. Now look at his living record. Am I reading it right? Rooming houses . . . shared apartments . . . annual turnovers. Where do they fall?"

Crighton examined them slowly. "Changing neighborhoods. Lots of inner city."

"Where is he now? This is the latest."

"That's quite respectable. He's well out Massachusetts Avenue, just above the embassies. That's as much an aberration as the rest. You're suggesting he's come into money?"

"It crossed my mind."

"Could be."

George asked, "Where is Jefferson University Hospital?"

"It used to be very respectable, but it got caught in the sixties riots and the area around it is a disaster. In the past couple of years, though, it's started up the other side, and it's increasingly Hispanic now."

"Is it? Purple cars," he said absently.

"That's the lot," Carson said, "but I say with my usual humility, I think I did splendidly, and if you notice, my hat is off. It is off to you, sir. I would never have thought of this approach."

"I was no surer than you were, but it seemed worth a try."

"Now, Mr. George," said Crighton, "it is definitely your turn. While we've been working our mouths, you've been grinding the brain. What is up?"

George grinned paternally and pulled a rumpled set of note sheets out of his pocket. "I have papers too. Unfortunately, these are just glorified doodles, but I say with modesty equal to Steve's: I know who killed Karl Vandermann."

"The hell you say!" shouted Carson.

"It has a few small holes in it, but I approached it in much the way you were moving your call slips, Steve. If you take everything we know about that group and line it up in different scenarios, the easiest one to swallow is the following."

George shifted his chair to face them more comfortably and leaned across the table.

"I give you your friend Mr. Merton."

"Are you hanging it on him?" Carson asked.

"I am. I narrowed it down to him by elimination and then built it back up by circumstance.

"First, we have to recognize that whoever did it might have hired an executor, but I don't believe Vandermann thought it was going to be done that way, and as egocentric as this bunch is, I don't think any of them would put their own safety in the hands of an outsider—an outsider who could either blackmail them at some later date, or betray them to buy his own way out of trouble. I think we have to assume that Vandermann was killed by one of the Executive Committee as he himself expected.

"I then matched opportunity, personality, motive, style, and apparent fiscal status of each, and although I could build a few elements against each of them, I found I could build a *complete* case against poor Mr. Merton. The problem is, the entire edifice is circumstantial, and we are going to have to devise some stratagem to get him to betray *himself. That* is the real challenge in this instance.

"But first, the case. Is this convincing?

"We hear that Merton has been with the group from the first. Why? Possibly because Vandermann really needed an accountant to keep the records. Possibly he needed an accountant who was a bit flexible with the rules to help with the tax corners. In any event, Merton comes on. But he is dreadfully below caste. Half the group are well-heeled economic aristocrats and the other half are over-educated intellectuals and Merton is considered beneath everyone's dignity.

"So this gives him great distress. Time passes, his own image of himself as a well-fixed entrepreneur is continually eroded. His jobs are marginal and their turnover abrades his self-image. He finally decides to move from questionable activities to outright theft—he knows coins and he decides to steal them.

"This is not as easy as I would have originally supposed. The coins are enormously valuable, buyers are abundant, he's a recognized collector, probably will have no trouble at all unloading them, but stealing them in the first place proves to be exceptionally difficult. Why? Because everyone who owns any of them expects them to be stolen and apparently the first thing they do is slam them into a vault. When are they out? Apparently at lecture time and to show off before friends. Hitting them when friends are there is little more than raw chance, but club programs are realistic targets. We find that Brother Merton as club secretary is given constant reports of who will have coins out where. He has the whole area to choose from—Lieutenant Price's thirty-five jurisdictions of which I will speak later. He can pick by kind of coin, he can pick by geography, a veritable spectrum, a palette of cash freshly drawn from the safe deposit vaults of our nation's capital!

"And what kinds does he select? English, if we are to believe the computer. Not U.S. Not German. Not Greek or Roman. Why English? Because half this coin game seems to be knowing what's valuable and what isn't. His own specialty seems to be Victorian, but I suspect the books the Queen's in will have something on all the English coins. He's on familiar ground.

"So my guess is we'll find him picking a target, say, once a month, in quite disparate places, almost certainly in different police jurisdictions, and he knocks them off one at a time in a fairly structured manner. My guess is that the kind of household that can afford rare coins is pretty square and pretty affluent. I'll bet he goes in, holds a gun to the owners, puts them in chairs where he immobilizes them quickly with handcuffs—beats a rope for sure— and collects the family *silver*. The plate. I'll bet in every case the coins are treated as afterthoughts that just happen to have been around by pure bad luck when the silver was taken. Our friend then throws it all into a brilliant purple, highly identifiable car he uses for the projects, drives the car back to the garage he rents somewhere near the hospital, moves the silver to his own pale blue Volkswagen, and goes home to his high rise on—where was it? Mass Ave.? And thus endeth the lesson for that month. Something attempted, something done has earned a night's repose. Longfellow. How does that seize you?"

They both burst into laughter.

"Hoo boy!" said Carson. "You started off so firmly on fact and spiraled right out into space. Circumstantial, he says! Hah!"

George grinned but said, somewhat defensively, "But you'll have to admit it all fits."

"It fits—providing that two-thirds of your guessed assumptions prove to be true."

Crighton smiled and said, "Where you're tricky, sir, is that you keep sprinkling in things we know are really so, along with a dozen that might be, but you use the same voice for both kinds."

"And he accuses me of jumping from what ought to be to what is!"

"Needless to say," George replied, "I am deeply hurt by both of your suspicions—but I'd have been disappointed if I hadn't gotten them. No, my strongest case is simply that while I could put together similar scenarios for the others, this one fits so well."

"What's the purple car and Chicano bit?" Crighton asked.

"Insurance, maybe?" said George. "I presume he wanted to put together a consistent, easy to identify and easy to remember character—one as wildly different from his own colorless self as possible, so if he was ever witnessed it would take the pursuers off in a wildly different direction. If the hospital's in the middle of the Hispanic slums, he could shuck the stereotype very easily."

Carson said, "All right. You've accounted for the sixteen thefts. How about the murder? I presume you make the tie to Vandermann by assuming that Vandermann found out what was going on. Merton then decides to kill him in the same way the thefts were done so it will look like just another of the string of silver burglaries."

"Correct. The more I work with it, the surer I am I'm right. But that's enough for now." George straightened up and said, "Let's call it a night. I'm going back to the club and make a list of all the . . . shall we call them 'weak spots'? . . . in my hypothesis, and I shall try them on Madame Lehman at the crack of dawn. I would be choked with gratitude if you two would put your young minds to the question of how we can either prove our guess or get Merton to prove it for us. Okay? Crighton, can you take me home?"

Crighton dropped the men off in sequence, and each of the team set themselves to think creatively. Indeed, the plan would have been a total success except for a single flaw.

When Edward George called Alexa Lehman at breakfast time, her first response to his salutation was a horrified, "Haven't you heard? They found Merton shot to death—handcuffed to his study chair."

8

"AND FRANKLY, SIR, I'M TERRIFIED," ALEXA Lehman said, with an intensity that chilled Edward George. "I don't think there is a shadow of a doubt that whatever Karl Vandermann had discovered is behind all this, and somebody is proceeding to kill us one after another, coldly and deliberately. The terrifying thing about it is that unless we can find out what Karl knew we can't even defend ourselves. What is it? Revenge? Preservation? Greed? I have been wracking my brains to think what the pattern could be. How do we all link? What is the common thread? I am not the least afraid of death. I have dealt with that since I was a target in a crumbling Reich, but I always knew who the enemy was and why he was a threat to me. This inability to build a rational chain is the most threatening thing that has ever happened to me."

George groped for a response. Her concern was only added to his own. Could he himself have caused Merton's death? Had Crighton or Steve talked to anyone? Had he inadvertently added the two

65

young people to the murderer's list? An icy thought struck him.

"Alexa, is everyone else accounted for? Are the others all right?"

"I've talked to Robert Charter and Barrow. I don't know about Eleanor York."

"Quickly. You call her and see that she is fully apprised of what has happened and suggest that she should be concerned about her own safety. I want to talk to my two young friends. I'll call you back as soon as I've . . . I've . . . Yes."

He hung up and hurriedly fanned his address book. He had no idea how to reach Steve Carson, but he could find Crighton at the library. He was searching for its number when he realized the Werner-Bok would not even open for another hour. Steve was in a rooming house or something, he recalled, but Crighton had her own apartment. She would be in the phone book. He found the book and then her number and dialed as quickly as stiffening hands could cope.

"Hello?" she said.

"Crighton! Edward George here. Are you all right?"

"Sure. What's the matter?"

"Look. Is there anyone in the apartment with you? If there is, say, 'I'll be in the library at the usual time.' "

"Uh? You've lost me. You know I have a roommate? Janet—Janet Jordan. Does she count?"

"Look. I'm sorry. I'm not making sense. That Merton fellow has been killed—just like Vandermann. I'm terrified that whoever is doing it is eliminating people who . . . we don't know what. Are you all right? There's no one holding a gun on you or anything?"

"Oh, boy. No. Nothing. Janet's in the shower . . . at least I think it was Janet . . . No, no, I saw her. We're okay."

"All right. Look, I'll call back with the details, but I've got to get in touch with Steve. Have you talked to him today?"

"Hardly."

"Can you give me his number? I want to be sure he's all right. And you—be very careful. Don't take any chances. Keep the door locked and don't let anyone in. Go out with your roommate. I'll call you at the library later today."

He roused Carson from a thickened sleep and after assuring himself of his safety brought him up to date to the extent of his own knowledge.

"Ummm," said Carson. "Is there a prayer that this is simply the

66

thing Merton was afraid of—that some thug would assume that everybody in that club had a million dollars lying about and . . . No, wait. Forget that. That doesn't make sense, does it? This isn't another silver robbery. This is another murder. A copy of the last one. Yeah, it's got to be a pattern. Was anything stolen?"

"I haven't heard any of the details, and I'm off now to get them. I'll call Crighton as soon as I know what's going on and you can keep in touch with her."

"Vandermann said someone was going to kill him, apparently because he had solved some kind of puzzle," Carson said. "Had Merton solved the same puzzle? Was *he* the puzzle? How do you tie the two together?"

"That seems to be what's bothering Alexa Lehman—her inability to get a rational, logical linkage among the events. There are a lot of things we need to know before we can speculate with any intelligence. What are your plans for the day?"

"Up to you. You're still on my forty-eight-hour allotment! Got any orders?"

"Bless you. Yes, if you can stay with me, you're much needed. In fact, time would seem to be doubly important now. It would appear that Vandermann 'found out' something, and was killed for it. Apparently Merton 'found out' something, and twenty-four hours later he was killed. I'm terrified that 'X' will think one of us has 'found out' whatever it is and eliminate us without our ever knowing we knew it!

"If you could get back to that CRT as quickly as you can, I think it would be of great merit. Bring up the sixteen stories and see if they tell us anything—a pattern or a purpose we haven't seen. We'll use Crighton as the crossover point, so be sure she knows where you are at all times. I'm going to see Madame Lehman and try to get some hard edges put on some blurred reports. In the meantime, be careful. Keep your door locked and try not to be alone if you can help it. Okay?"

"Got you. I'll start on the stories, and wait for you at the Werner-Bok."

George broke off the conversation and called Alexa Lehman again.

"Did you get Miss York?"

"Yes. She is accounted for—and warned."

"How did she take the news?"

67

"Of Merton's death or her danger?"

"Good point. They are different, aren't they? All right, both."

"Of Merton's passing, conventionally. She said all the proper things. Of the possibility that she might be next, quietly. I don't know why, but I was expecting something else."

"Ummm. Very well. Madame Lehman, I presume you will not be too surprised when I say I think you and I had better talk. I want to know whatever you do about the circumstances of Merton's death, and I could use a bit more information about yourself. If we're still speaking after all that, then I think the two of us should rethink the linkages here. We automatically assumed we were involved in the coin matter. Could it have been something else, and if so, what? That is the agenda. At the outset, are you willing to be candid with me about these matters?"

"I am delighted you're taking this seriously," she said. "Incidentally, I appreciate your not having said, 'You got me into this,' but I recognize that I did and I am under great obligation to you. I will be happy to tell you anything I know. Would you like to come here?"

"Thank you. Is there any better place? I fear I might feel somewhat intimidated on your own grounds, but I should imagine a men's club would be equally alien for you. That leaves Gadsby's Tavern, I suppose. No. That's clumsy. Very well. I accept your offer. May I come now?"

Alexa Lehman's apartment proved to be magnificent—as George had expected it to be. Soft carpeting flowed from one wide room to another; glass walls opened onto balconies which in turn overlooked Rock Creek Park, and the feel of comfortable opulence was everywhere. Contrary to his expectations, however, there were no antiques, no artworks, only rich, well-selected furniture that tied together in a sense of comfort. No single piece demanded individual attention to itself.

"You have a beautiful home here," George said. "What a sublime combination of elegance and taste." He looked around, nodding. "But no objets d'art. Any special reason?"

"I guess I never really believed I was safe. My whole life was spent either in flight or being ready to fly. For years I saw to it that there was nothing I could not leave behind without its tearing out a part of me. My husband was Jewish—he was the youngest department head at the University of Dresden—and he was seized in

1938. I never saw him again. Since my own bloodline and pedigree were acceptable, I was never imprisoned, but I was suspect throughout the war and was moved from one town to another. I was in Poland when the Eastern Front began to collapse, and the Russians moved faster than we civilians could retreat so we were overrun. That left me on the Russian side at the end, and it took two more years to get back to what was left of Dresden. Of course Dresden ended up on the Communist side, so it was not until the early fifties that I got to the West by way of Austria, Switzerland, and England. As you can see, I was . . . shall we say, mobile? . . . and though I really lived very well most of the time, it was no time for possessions."

"I find the thought of such dissolution . . . anarchism . . . terrifying. How could you 'live well' amid such chaos?" George asked.

She laughed casually, seating herself across from him. "Unfortunately the assumption is that we all did it by selling our bodies." She chuckled. "I say with some pride that at the time I was quite attractive enough to have been able to do so if it had been necessary—but of course it never really was. There is always need for intelligence, style, and a willingness to work. Long before the present fashion there were jobs for women in banking and commerce, and these sustained me in Germany and Austria. I worked for the Russians during the Occupation—I started as a translator and quickly became a go-between for the German provincial governments and the Communists. I sat in endless committee meetings, I negotiated tax agreements and currency agreements. I was the 'representative' to this and the 'controller' of that and ultimately I got into the international banking world and things became much easier—trans-borders, as it were."

"Did you come to America with the World Bank or something?"

"No, I was sent here to report *on* the World Bank for three houses in Munich, and then I did the same—reporting on the currency situation—for a number of Swiss banks until the seventies. A few years ago I 'retired,' I guess you'd say—at least I left off cashing other people's checks and began to enjoy myself."

"It's clear you have earned it."

"I suppose so. In my business there are the kinds of people who report what is going on and let someone else take actions and make decisions on the strength of their reports, and there are people who not only make the reports but play the game themselves. The myth among my friends was always that the latter were suspect. Either you'd begin to warp your reports to protect your own interests, or you'd be so preoccupied with your own needs, you'd subconsciously see what you wanted to see. I always felt that was fallacious. I reported what I saw and I used my own money to take advantage of it. I always believed it made my reports more conscientious—it always reminded me that my words were going to affect other people's actions. I say with very little modesty, I was right most of the time. What you see here," she waved her hand around the comfort of the room, "is the result of using a salaried employee's paycheck in an intelligent way."

"You collect gold coins, don't you? Did they contribute to this?" George imitated her gesture.

"No, oddly enough. They started as insurance. In the early days when I was really living from hand to mouth, I would always put back a tiny bit in case of disaster. I'd buy gold coins because, just like in the motion pictures, they can be carried on your person, and a very small volume represents a great deal of money. I always thought that either I could fall back on the gold coins if I got into trouble or I could sell them if I was safe and make money on them." She laughed. "Neither one of them happened. I never got into such trouble I had to use them to survive, and as I got more secure, I didn't have to give them up and they simply became more and more valuable. I have used them as security for speculations on several occasions, but I rarely have sold any of them—just added through the years."

"Are the coins modern?"

"No, they're antique like most of the others in Karl's club. A modern gold piece like an Elizabeth II sovereign is worth about fifty dollars, but the same-sized piece from Elizabeth I is worth a bit over three thousand. So at the first, I bought historical coins because I could carry more money on me. After that I just kept on because they are so romantic. I was quite carried away with Louis XIV and Catherine of Russia, I recall." She laughed. "Ah, a fine gold strike is a beautiful piece of art. You know gold does not 'age'—it never looks old. A Florentine florin—or a ducat of Venice—is as brilliant and shiny today as it was nearly a thousand years ago when it was made."

70

"I didn't know that. Where did you meet Karl Vandermann?"

"He was a financial reporter for the Amsterdam *Telegraaf*, and we traded thoughts at Bretton Woods and Lugano and the Hague— all the early monetary conferences. In those days we thought the agreements would solve the fiscal problems of the world for all time."

"Sounds incredibly boring."

"Not so. It was exciting and hopeful—and we now know, incredibly naïve."

"I envy his having known you then. Speaking only from a natural jealousy, dare I ask if there was ever any ... personal ... relationship?"

"Your gallantry is not sufficient cover, sir. What you are asking is, How closely were we involved in the light of our recent troubles? I was fond of him and we reduced the boredom that occurs between plenary sessions, but I never expected anything to come of it. Naturally I would say, 'I think he was more interested than I was.' " She paused and then laughed. "That is a marvelous phrase, isn't it? We probably owe it to Eve."

"You arrived before he did?"

"Oh, I'd lost track of him years before. I came here and he went into teaching in Europe. He turned up at Georgetown and we made contact through mutual friends."

"But thanks to the club he invented, you saw him monthly— maybe weekly?"

"You sound like a jealous husband. While what you say is true, its connotation is flawed. And its implication. May I get you a cup of coffee?" she asked suddenly.

"Why, yes. I would like that."

She touched a silent button he had not seen on an end table, and to his surprise a uniformed maid came in carrying an ornate silver tray. She set it on the coffee table and raised her eyebrows at the hostess who nodded, and the maid withdrew silently.

"Will you try one of the rolls? Peach? Cinnamon?"

George laughed. "By God, you do live in style, Madame. Yale was never like this. Whatever you recommend. I am in your hands. Cream and sugar, please."

Once served, he picked up the conversation quickly. "How was Mr. Merton discovered? And when was it? This morning?"

"Yes. One of the men on his floor wished to ride into town with

71

him, so he had gone to ask for transportation and found the door ajar. He pushed it open and walked in, expecting to find Merton waiting for the paper or something. Instead he was sitting at his desk, his hands handcuffed through the rungs of the chair back behind him, and a bullet hole in the center of his forehead."

"How long had he been dead?"

"Apparently it happened late last evening. Before midnight."

"Did no one hear a shot?"

"I learn that is the price we pay for luxury apartments. The walls and doors are so thick to ensure privacy that a shot is sufficiently muffled it can be confused with a television program."

"Did anyone hear a noise they thought was television?"

"I'm afraid you're approaching a level of specificity that exceeds my information source."

George smiled. "Yes, what is your information source, if I may ask?"

She laughed. "Margaret Belmont. Who else? Margaret lives five floors above Mr. Merton, but she has at least one friend on every floor, and the rumor tree had the news throughout the building in less than five minutes. Madge Elkins told Ann Eicholtz, who told . . . and so forth."

"Ummm," said George. "Fortunately, I have a friend in the police department who is supposed to get back tonight. With any luck, I can dredge up some details from him.

"Madame Lehman . . . Alexa. I am going to spend the day talking to the other members of your club. I want to search for linkages. We assumed the coins or the coin club were the common denominator. If it were to prove this was not so, what options do we have? How else are you people tied together? Help me with this one and I'll leave you."

"Dr. George . . . Edward. I hope we can meet on some occasion when we can speak of something other than this horrible murder— these murders, I must say now." She shuddered. "But linkages. As you know, this has concerned me too. So far, I have toyed with the following." She counted off on her fingers. "One. The school where Karl taught. Charter is a fellow teacher, Paul Barrow has given guest lectures to Karl's seminars, Eleanor York was a student.

"Two. Europe. Karl knew me in Germany and Paul in England. Three. Money. We are all hoarding very expensive forms of dollars.

72

Only Jerry Merton had a modest collection. Eleanor's is very large for a person her age. The ones belonging to the rest of us make us very wealthy indeed."

"Even Barrow? I sensed he was just a salaried employee."

"He may have been, but his Roman materials add up to several hundred thousand dollars. He simply does not spend his money on himself or on seeable things."

"Great heavens," said George. "Can you accumulate that kind of money on a government salary? Is there money in his family?"

"No, to your first question. I am sure his discretionary income never exceeded five thousand dollars a year in the past three decades. I don't know about family money, and if it were anyone but Paul Barrow, I would have to say I don't know about black market activities or influence money. Both of those are all too easy for foreign service officers to meet. Fortunately, there has been a very high level of professionalism in that corps.

"If I may move on," she said, "I note Number Four, sex. Assuming that cherchezing la femme has not been outlawed in our time, I note that Paul Barrow was once in love with Eleanor York, Vandermann had her in his classes, and Merton made endless passes at her in my sight and apparently out of it. Before I force you to think of some tactful way of asking, Karl Vandermann at one time found me attractive and Paul Barrow looks on me as one of the few women he has ever known 'he can talk to.' Not only has this been a mixed blessing all my life, but I can never be sure it is not a slur on my femininity."

"Are you suggesting that you have not attracted Dr. Charter or Brother Merton?"

"Charter would like to attract Miss York, but only because he assumes that all Brown men who wear vests are irresistible to all women and Miss York's physical attributes make her a woman in spades. Mr. Charter is baffled by me. I do not fit into the stereotypes he acquired at Brown. I say acquired because I doubt if they teach them anything there. What they know they seem to absorb through their skin. I did indeed fascinate Mr. Merton. When he looked into my eyes he saw two large, endlessly negotiable dollar signs. One in each pupil. I was a walking credit line for the poor man." She laughed. "I wouldn't think of letting him use money I had worked so hard to get. He was contemptible. But I am speaking ill of the

73

dead. Those are the four links I could see easily. I will think about others that may not be so apparent. But these should give you something to start on."

George got his legs under him and stood up. "Madame Lehman, you have given me far more than a start. You know, you are indeed as attractive as you think you are. You are also exhausting. I find that it is bad enough trying to keep up with your thinking, but the real energy loss is effort wasted in trying not to look like a fool in front of you. You force me to double-think everything I say, and I don't even do that for myself—much less for anyone else."

She laughed with obvious delight. "How gracefully you flatter me, sir. And what a shame we had to meet in such unfortunate circumstances."

"Bless you again," he said. "I will be calling you for more help, soon, I know."

Once on the street he asked the doorman to get him a cab and looked at his watch. Ten o'clock. Not bad. A quick stop with Crighton and then to look in some corners not yet explored by anyone.

9

NOTWITHSTANDING A FUNERAL PROCESSION coming out of the National Cathedral, a demonstration at the mosque, and two sight-seeing buses with locked bumpers by the OAS Building, George reached the Werner-Bok by ten thirty. As they approached the Constitution Avenue entrance, the taxi driver asked, "Which side do you want?"

"Actually the Mall, but I can walk around it faster than you can drive. This will do fine."

He paid the driver and stood on the sidewalk for a moment. Now what? he thought. He decided he was not yet ready to see Crighton and wanted a moment to collect his thoughts. The morning was cool, but it was brilliantly clear with a blue sky made even bluer by the white of the Capitol dome down the Mall to his left. He decided to seek a park bench and think about his troubles.

He strode purposefully around the building and was delighted to find several empty seats across from the library's fountain. He crossed the Drive and seated himself in the sunniest spot he could find. What indeed? he thought.

The Renaissance façade of the library distracted him for a moment and he let his eyes trace the lines of flowing staircases, monumental piazzas, and granite columns. He examined carved busts perched over every window arch and wondered at the massive grilles set across each basement opening. By God, they knew how to build them, he thought. Could we still do it? he wondered. We could obviously design one, but do we have the artisans? The money? The time? He looked down the Mall to his right where the National Gallery sat in serene simplicity—the aesthetic antithesis of the Werner-Bok, yet equally satisfactory. No, more so. He recalled Da Vinci's story about the white room without doors or windows but open to the sky. If you could only see one shape painted on a wall for all eternity, which shape would it be? The story said not the circle, the square, or the straight line. Not the spiral or the rectangle but a triangle, Da Vinci maintained. If you had to look at one façade forever, which would be the best? Italian Renaissance, Greek Classic, or red brick Georgian? For interest and novelty, the Renaissance, he decided. For working and living with, the Georgian. But for all eternity, he thought, you'd have the best chance to avoid madness with a nice, white, Greek temple. Well, he smiled to himself, having got that settled, where am I on my more immediate problem?

First, he thought, I'm in fair shape with time. I'm still within my two-day schedule, and we've got a good deal of data to work with. Unfortunately, except for the discredited Merton hypothesis, there was no obvious or convincing pattern yet. But here he was optimistic. The chances for a breakthrough were good.

How about danger? Not good. Alexa was convinced the two deaths were the first of a series unless the murderer could be found and stopped. Was there really any reason to think there would be a third? Yes. With a single murder, there was very little chance there would be two. With two, there was a strong chance there would be three. Why? Because, apparently, whatever there was about Vandermann that required he be killed, there was about Merton too. What was it, again? Because they "knew too much"? If the killer had done something wrong and the victims knew what it was and were going to tell someone, it would explain why they had to be killed. Workable reason. But how about revenge? If the victims had done something wrong that had already damaged the killer, he would have reason to get even for the damage they had done him. In the first instance, it would be easy to have another death—someone else could "know." In the second? Yes, if a third person had shared in the injustice . . . the "damage" . . . he would have to be killed too. Same conclusion. How did that go? If it is already raining today, the chance it will keep raining into tomorrow is greater than that it will be clear even if it's been raining for a week. Really? Or something. He laughed and shook his head. Where did that get him? he asked himself. That there were all too many reasons for a third person to be killed.

Then what was the linkage between One and Two that would help him anticipate who Three would be? And did he need to know Three more than he needed to know who the murderer himself was? Which should he concentrate on? Who would be the next or who was doing it? Endless chain. Circular knot. Forget that approach.

No, the secret was the pattern. What events? What reasons? What style made a logical pattern? You find that, and you'll find all your answers. What pattern . . . ? He started to order his thoughts again when he interrupted himself. No. This is unproductive. You still don't know enough. It's time to find out what you don't know. He got to his feet, felt for his wallet, and started back across the street for the Werner-Bok.

He found Crighton busily laying out her day, and he briefed her quickly on what he had learned from Alexa Lehman. A phone call interrupted their conversation, and he stared at her as she dealt with the query. The very personification of bright-eyed, stylish intelligence, he thought. The vigor of youth, how attractive and how reassuring. She completed the call with efficiency and humor, and turned to him as she hung up the phone.

"Dammit! Here we're trying to solve two murders and the phone is business as usual. Doesn't it know . . . ?"

"No. It is right," George said. "As an old-line administrator, I'm feeling guilty about using your time on this distraction. Let me bother you with just one more thing and I'll get out of your hair.

"Re those murders. I'm convinced we've got to know more about those people in the coin club. The linkages. Vandermann said one of them was going to kill him and, sure enough, he's dead. And until we learn something more than we have now, we've got to assume one of them did it. So I'm off to talk to that Barrow fellow—the civil servant. As sour as he's supposed to be, maybe he can see the scene with more detachment than the rest of us. Next, when I see Steve, I want to sic him on to Charter—and that leaves Sister York to you. I don't want to waste your working day, but if there is any way you could grill the lady in the evening . . ."

"Easy. We'd already left it we were going to get together and talk about the situation. With the Merton murder, I can speed it up— probably tonight. What am I looking for?"

"I pretty much leave that up to you. We need relationships . . . history . . . motivations—anything that will give us some pattern. What does she know about the people on that committee that might tell us something? What's going on here!"

"Good. No strain. I'll float it free. Steve is up at the computer reading those coin robbery stories, and we're due to have lunch together. Is there anything you want me to tell him—or are you going to see him yourself?"

"No, there's no sense in my wasting his time now. If he can think of any way to meet with Charter, have him pursue the same sort of thing you're after with York. Tell him to be sure *you* know where he is at all times. I'll be back at closing time to see where we all stand. All right?"

"Great. I'll see that Steve is here and waiting."

"Then I'm off. Concentrate on your work. Don't give these murders a second thought till you're on your own time. Understand?"

Crighton laughed. "You are, of course, kidding. You talk like a boss. I thought you were retired."

They grinned at each other and George slipped into the hall.

"Bless you, sir," said Edward George, "for meeting me on such short notice." He and Paul Barrow, late of his President's foreign service, were comfortably slouched in an eighteenth-century booth in Gadsby's Tavern. Still-frosted pewter mugs of beer sat on the table in front of them.

"I was pleased to have the opportunity to talk to you," Barrow said. "That odd meeting we had upstairs yesterday has caused me considerable concern. I was afraid you might have taken away some improper impressions."

"I share your frustration with that exchange. Let's act like it

78

never happened. Square One. But before we get involved in the murders, I wanted to ask you about that challenge . . . the charge . . . Dr. Charter threw at you about your pessimism. Was it fair? Would you like to rebut?"

"Not necessarily. Essentially he was right. I don't know whether our experience has led us to different conclusions, or our natural prejudices have given us different experiences, but we do indeed believe in different worlds. Charter is preoccupied with the rise of the underdeveloped countries. He finds the mere creation of a new, 'free' nation good. He would have us believe so long as the locals rule, they can do no wrong. Arrant nonsense. I think even he will admit it's a hell of a lot crummier to live in one of those liberated countries now than it was when they were under the European yoke, but he will always say, 'they'll improve—their future is all before them.' He then assumes that by definition if it's a future it will get better and better. I tell you, *my* world is the West and in *my* lifetime I have seen it crest and it is now deteriorating. My experience says the world we know is going to get increasingly painful in our lifetime and in the lifetime of our children. His experience makes him believe that in Africa, for instance, every day in every way is going to be better and better."

"And you don't think it will?"

"Christ, no. Africa is in for a century of territorial wars, palace coups, bankruptcies, starvation, and plague. Literally. But the young liberals now think there's no way to go but up. Bullshit. There is one hell of a lot of down they haven't even seen yet."

"Charter accused you of liberalism—an implied naïveté . . ."

"Yes, and he was right there too. We all genuinely thought that the whole world was filled with nice people like us who wanted to live in the same nice way and do the same nice things we did. We never realized what a delicate, incredibly good thing we had going in America in the fifties and sixties. It's the Roman Empire all over again."

"Do you think there's an analogy between Rome's Fall and your present . . . decline of the West?"

"Frighteningly so."

"Anything special, or general miasma?"

Barrow smiled wanly. "I guess I'd vote general miasma." He drank a substantial part of his mug, and wiped his lips. "What killed off Rome? The scholars used to think there was a 'something'

79

that did it—immorality or inflation . . . too much government. Too much Christianity? Everybody had his pet theory but none was really convincing. The great universal explanations make much better sense—Toynbee or even Spengler are much more persuasive. They think that civilizations do indeed have a youth—vigorous and optimistic; they have a middle age—effective and efficient; and an old age in which everything simply runs down and dies. Absolutely inevitable. There's nothing can be done to avoid it."

"But then aren't Charter's developing countries on the way up—young and vigorous?"

"Oh, no, just being young doesn't ensure success—it's simply that you can't be successful unless you're young. It was the Roman Empire's youth that made it possible to raise its culture—and incidentally, the 'oppressed colonies' of the Romans were almost all better off thanks to the Empire than the free tribes outside the wall. The only African and Asian countries that are going to make it today are the client states. Freedom in that mess is suicidal. But there will be endless young societies that will die for every young one that will survive. The telling point is that there's not a single example of an old society that has successfully regenerated."

"Not even China?"

"Fair question. I'm not yet sure what that experiment means."

"But doesn't the 'melting pot' idea give us an out? The American society has surely been young and strong, but it was essentially people and traditions from the 'old' world. It wasn't the Indians and the Eskimos who made it. Can't we keep our youth by absorbing endless outside cultures?"

"Hah! The way the Chicanos are pouring in, you'll soon be able to see."

"Yes, but I'll bet they and the Orientals and the Arabs that are coming will rejuvenate the society."

Barrow laughed. "You sound like a nineteenth-century immigration officer. My guess is you're kidding yourself."

"But you sound like a Victorian imperialist. Were you always so strong on paternalism?"

"Hardly! I had a major role in kicking the British out of Ceylon. They should hang me for it. A fine, healthy, law-abiding, and vigorous society has been reduced to a primitive slum in one generation. Under the British, a child had a chance to go to school, get a job, live three-score years, and die with the satisfaction of knowing his own sons and daughters would have an even better chance than he did. Today—just twenty years from independence— the schools are closed, the life-span is vastly shortened, crime is endemic, and almost a third of the nation is unemployed and living on bowls of doled swill. My God. And all in the name of freedom."

"I can see why Dr. Charter . . . what did he say, you'd have me cutting my wrists in fifteen minutes? I do believe he's right!"

Barrow chuckled quietly. "Don't let it worry you. That's the great advantage of people's short memory. It won't be long before no one can recall how good it used to be and they won't feel put upon at all."

George shook his head and shuddered. "I'm sorry I brought it up!" He laughed and straightened up on the bench. "I'm intrigued with the way a foreign officer thinks. I suspect you are trained to generalize and forecast. Is that true . . . fair?"

"Yes. I presume you mean in contrast to decide and act. Yes, that's very much the case. When you're running a post, you expect the clerks at the bottom to deal with things that require activity. The senior personnel spend eighty percent of their time—maybe ninety—trying to figure out what's going on in the country and trying to anticipate what will happen next."

"Good. That's what I thought. That thought pattern could be of great use in our present problem. I don't think I'm giving away any great secret when I say that Karl Vandermann told me he thought someone on the Executive Committee was going to kill him. And he *was* killed. Then, at least to *my* astonishment, Merton was killed too. Surely two more disparate figures could not be found in any group. Why Merton? And will that end it, or are the rest of you threatened?"

"I don't think there's any doubt we're potential targets," Barrow replied.

"Do you know on what grounds? Why? How?"

"No. No, I genuinely don't."

"Is there any one of the group that you distrust or fear? Personally?"

"Merton. I think he was totally without principle. A-moral, not immoral. But he's dead."

"He is indeed," said George. "So that leaves Charter, Eleanor York, and Alexa Lehman. Scarcely a threatening group."

"Oh, I don't know. Charter finds me almost as contemptible as I

81

did Merton. Eleanor York is a cold-blooded product of modern woman, and Alexa Lehman would commit murder just to amuse herself."

"Lehman? Really?"

"Oh, yes. I can picture her setting up danger and deliberately getting as close to exposure as possible just to see if she could control it . . . manipulate the characters and the scene."

"Someone told me that there was once a personal relationship between you and Eleanor York. Is it appropriate for me to ask . . ."

"I am quite willing to talk about it. Yes, I was once very much in love with her. We met in one of Karl Vandermann's seminars. He asked me to give some lectures on Roman archaeology to one of his senior classes. She was there and I had never been so struck with brains and beauty in my life—indeed, although I had always associated with many women, no single one had ever seized my total attention. But she did. Oh, my yes. You know, there is nothing so desirable . . . so sexy . . . as an intelligent, beautiful woman. Those gray eyes, a mind that runs way ahead of the group, the poise and challenge of a personality that has always dominated any relationship—lovely, Dr. George. Lovely." His eyes ceased to focus on George and seemed to be looking back into his memory.

"Did you tell her so?" George asked.

"I did indeed. We had a passionate affair. I was between my Paris and London assignments and involved in what to her was the most glamorous part of Washington social life. It was a fair bargain. I gave her access and I knew I was bringing the most beautiful woman to any affair. Affair. Interesting word—ours was an affair only because that's what she wanted. I wanted to marry her. She was absolutely right, of course. What is there?—fifteen years?—between us?"

"She never . . ." George did not know how to avoid the cliché.

". . . led me on?" Barrow solved his problem. "Never in any way other than being there and being more desirable every day. I painted it all myself."

"How did it end?"

"Hah! On my good days I thought that I had made her a richer, fuller, more sensitive person. On my bad days I thought she had figured a way to visit all the local embassies in the company of a senior officer of the State Department with very little effort."

82

"When did the bad days start?"

"When I knew that I was being assigned to London and tried to force an acceptance from her."

"But when you came back?"

"It seemed . . . inappropriate."

"To her or to you?"

"Both. The fifteen years' difference that had seemed so minor to me when I was 'somebody,' forty, and exerting political power was apparent even to me when I was 'nobody,' fifty, and had retired from the foreign service."

"But she is in the coin club . . ."

"Yes, I introduced her to it when we were going together. She has continued her interest."

"Did you introduce her to coin collecting too?"

"Yes, we built her collection together."

"I understand it is very extensive now."

"It is indeed. She has acquired very wisely."

"But I hear yours is unusually fine too. How did you get started? Roman, is it?"

"Nothing dramatic. I had spent thirty years specializing in Roman archaeology, and coins have always been very important to that. Both Roman and Greek sites have been rich in coinage and we've always used them to date the digs. The Greek coins are works of art. Magnificent. And the Roman coinage is so precise and workmanlike that it and architectural inscriptions are the best dating devices we have for the whole culture. When Hadrian became emperor, the Egyptians put his head on their coins and the British and the Macedonians and the Numidians, et cetera, et cetera. And then when Antoninus took over, the Egyptians put his head on their coins and the British and the Macedonians and the Numidians . . . and we have a single, uniform dating device that works in every part of the known world. This didn't occur again until Victoria, you know. Regina."

"Did you specialize in Hadrian?"

"Archaeologically, yes. Not as coins. I have the whole Roman series."

"But that is hundreds . . . maybe thousands . . . of coins!"

"Yes."

"But how could . . . weren't they . . . ?"

83

"I built most of my collection abroad when the pieces were mostly curiosities or souvenirs. They have just become valuable in the last two decades."

"Did you know Madame Lehman when you were overseas?"

"No. We met in the club."

"Well, you have been most kind to give me all this time. One final question. If you were in my shoes, how would you proceed now? What would you do next?"

"Nothing. Absolutely nothing."

"What?"

"Sir, I think you are fooling yourself with the thought these murders can somehow be solved rationally. I would leave the matter rigorously to the police. Ratiocination is delusive. Detached, objective police techniques are far more appropriate in this case. Indeed, proceeding as you are, I suspect the chance of your implicating an innocent figure is very great."

George was so startled by Barrow's attitude and admonition that he made no attempt to deal with it, and let the conversation come to an abrupt end. He said the necessary and expected words but by rote, and the two men parted.

Rather than returning at once to Washington, George walked deeper into colonial Alexandria until he came onto the open market square of colonial times now landscaped and serving as the center pivot of the city. He selected a comfortable bench, seated himself on it, and furrowed his brow. Wait just one damn minute, he said to himself. I misread that completely. What is important here? Which truth? He pursed his lips and summarized:

One. The last person who told me to leave well enough alone was Merton, and now Merton is dead. Is the reason Barrow is trying to drive me away the same reason that Merton had, toward the same end? And if so, what is it?

Or Two. What has been the most savage, most irrational motive for murder ever since Eden? Jealousy. The blind, unreasoning hurt and fury over the thought of the loved one in someone else's arms. Merton made endless passes at the beautiful Miss York. The beautiful Miss York stroked and fondled by the repellent hand of Merton. Who would care the most? Clearly Brother Barrow. And Merton is dead.

Now what have we learned here, George asked himself as he slumped down and began to work on it. What have we learned?

84

10

AT FIVE MINUTES AFTER TWELVE, STEVE Carson strode into Crighton's office.

"You're late," she said.

He put his hands over her ears, tilted her face up to his, and kissed her firmly on the mouth.

"Woman, you are a good thing," he said. "If it weren't for your lousy disposition . . ." He ran his hands up into her hair, made a wreck of her coiffure, and collapsed into the chair beside her desk.

"In my undergraduate days," he said, "I cursed the microfilm machine. I have been carsick in front of the New York *Times,* the Chicago *Tribune,* and a hundred blurred Illinois papers on a thousand reels of microform. But none of it was as bad as those goddamn cathode ray tubes. It's the fill and clear, fill and clear. You can't not look until the lines are complete, but reading green text as it crawls across a soggy screen is the end of the world. Oh, for a clay tablet and a faded scroll!" Crighton rose and went to a filing cabinet to return a mound of folders and as she shoved in the drawer he said, "Woman, you have the most perfectly proportioned bottom of any female in the world. What a contribution you make to a scene. When are you going to marry me?"

"When you make a decent living and give up your preoccupation with women's behinds."

"May I die first. I have made a life's career of this specialty and I have never regretted a single moment." He stared at the ceiling and smiled with remembered satisfactions. "Did you know that I played the trombone when I was in high school? Very well too. And why, you ask, the trombone? Because they came right after the drum majorettes in the marching band. Marvelous decision. I learned more between the 'Stars and Stripes Forever' and 'Colonel Bogey' than I ever did in biology class."

"You're disgusting."

"Nonsense. If I hadn't examined all those others, how would I be able to appreciate the sublime perfection of yours? But there is one thing that has always worried me. What is the correlation between a beautiful bottom and a handsome face? If you come upon a girl and are inspired from the rear, what are the odds that her face will be equally good from the front?"

"I could weep. Fifty years of the Movement, and there are still creeps like you out of jail. Are you going to feed me or not?"

"I am. I am so punchy from those machines I thought we should go to the open air. How does two box lunches from the Hirshhorn grab you?"

"It makes better sense than you usually do. Come on."

They struggled into their coats and headed for the Mall.

The Hirshhorn Museum of Art sits across the greensward from the Werner-Bok and belongs to local Washingtonians like all the other museums belong to the tourists. It is new, eclectic, and an institution with a sense of humor. It has an enormous collection that seems to change every week, and from Carson's point of view, its most valuable feature is an outdoor kiosk that sells gourmet box lunches. These are intended to be eaten in the sunken sculpture garden buried in the Mall out front. While the museum stands proud and conspicuous, the sculpture garden is so effectively camouflaged that most tourists never learn it's there. It thus serves as a refuge for retired esthetes, government workers, and camera-men who think they've died and gone to heaven.

86

The sculpture garden is a single-lens reflex owner's idea of Paradise. Each piece of imaginatively titled metal cries out to be photographed while lying on the ground, shot through a partner's legs, or reflected in the polish of the next piece of statuary, which in turn cries out to be photographed . . . and so on. Thus surrounded by the whir of focal plane shutters, the two young people found themselves a comfortable wall to lean on and distributed the contents of their packed lunches. A bronze Venus with an erector set for a womb provided a shelf to set the wine on.

"Artichokes and butter? I think they've overshot today," said Crighton. "Did those computer articles pan out at all?"

"Very nicely indeed," Carson replied. "The first thing that hit me was the fact that the stories were all from the regional . . . community papers. Nothing in the *Post* or *Star* at all. And then I got to thinking, the big sheets don't really report small crimes, do they? Except for particularly dramatic murders and bank robberies, the day-to-day sort of things that drive the taxpayer up the wall are never mentioned at all. Do you suppose that's because crimes are so common they're not really 'news,' or is it to keep the community from getting uptight? If we knew how really likely it was that we'd be robbed or mugged in any one day, we'd be walking paranoids."

"I do have a degree in journalism, you know," Crighton said, "but I've never heard the rationale on that one. In smaller papers, your police beat is high priority. I don't know about the metropolitan stuff. Their sales areas are so much larger than local interest, maybe they can't afford the space. The news hole is getting smaller all the time too."

"News hole?"

"What's left over for print after the ads are set in place."

"You mean a paper is made up with the ads in first and then the news goes in what's left?"

"You got it. Only the front page and the editorials are free. Management decides how much they can afford to waste on news and the editors know how much linage that leaves available. It never varies once the allocation is made."

"I thought you had big news days and little news days and the amount of news printed reflected it!"

"No difference. Watch it. A newspaper has just so much linage for news no matter what. You never reduce your advertising."

"Another girlish illusion shot down."

Crighton laughed. "So what did you learn?"

"Well, George was right when he guessed they were pretty standardized—the robberies. They followed a highly structured pattern. As we knew, they all fell on Saturdays or Sundays. They all fell in the evenings—after dark no matter what season it was—but never after eleven. Several times the car was noticed with the flames—no, several times the *flames* were noticed. Only once was the purple color or the car described—at least in the news stories."

Crighton shook her head. "Strange," she said. "What was the handcuff bit?"

"You couldn't really tell. In each case a single burglar dressed in coveralls rang the doorbell. When the door was opened he-she-or-it pointed a gun at whoever opened it, forced them into a chair, and made them put their arms through the back, where they were handcuffed. In those cases where there was more than one person in the house, he threatened to shoot the one that opened the door and then got everyone else down and handcuffed them all. He then searched the house himself, piled all the silver by the door, and just before he left, threw it into pillowcases he stole from the house."

"Why he-she-or-it?"

"No one seemed able to tell which. 'He' talked in a high voice with a thick Spanish accent. Both the size and the voice could have been a woman. The head was always covered with a stocking, and the feet wore canvas running shoes. No gender."

"Three of the victims were killed?"

"Right. Inexplicably. They were in the chairs, handcuffed, all the other elements were just like the rest, except they'd been shot in the center of their foreheads."

"I wonder if stuffing your head in a stocking really does disguise you. It's just barely possible that the three people who were shot were unlucky enough to recognize the burglar and say so. If Mr. George's 'hypothesis' had been true, the three might have remembered Merton from some kind of coin convention or something. May I shove your face in a stocking to see? I probably couldn't tell the difference—might even be an improvement."

Carson stuck out his tongue at her and said, "I've heard they sell panty hose by head size in the high-crime district."

Crighton laughed and asked, "How about the coins?"

"Rarely mentioned as such. The stories all stressed the theft of tea services or trays or sterling tableware. The coins were always sort of thrown in at the end line."

"Do you think it would be worth our time to try to get a list of what was taken? Would it tell us anything?"

"Good question. I feel like George did about those city directories. I doubt it, but I think we should know, if only to be able to forget it. Yeah, at some point we ought to try to get a list of the stolen property."

"I wonder if the police stations would have it in such detail? They're liable just to have 'various coins worth a thousand dollars.' Maybe we ought to consider interviewing some of the victims."

"Why don't you try that on Sister York? See if she thinks it would pay off. While you're at it, you might ask her about insurance on these things. Is it possible that these are like jewels and you can make more money hitting the insurance companies than you can trying to get someone to buy 'em back?"

"I'll see what she says. We're supposed to have supper together at her apartment."

"What a waste," Carson said. "Two unusually beautiful women . . ."

"You're doing it again."

"When *are* you going to marry me?"

"I never said I was."

"I know that, but you are exceptionally bright, have an unusual amount of taste and discrimination. There is no question you'll recognize I'm as good as there is available. The only problem is when? Do I have to stake out a cave and deliver fresh meat to you for a month to prove myself or something? How are you fixed for grails? Dragon head, lady?"

She grinned at him but did not reply.

"That's the curse of you self-sufficient women. We men fall madly and totally in love with you and we recognize that life without you is not worth living. We spend hours thinking of when we can see you and then the moment we part we start thinking about when we can see you again the next time. But we never cross your mind once a year. Do you ever wonder if I'm going to call? No! Do you ever think what it would be like if I got hit by a truck? Never! What happened to the woman who sat by the phone and prayed it would ring?"

Crighton laughed, and said, "You wouldn't want us if we were like that. It's our ability to take you or leave you alone that makes us attractive to you."

"Try me! Just once act delighted when I come in the room. Sit by the phone and pick it up on the first ring. Once! Just once!" He suddenly dropped to his knees in front of her and assumed the supplicant's pose. "Marry me! Please marry me."

Crighton laughed again and said, "Get up, you character. You're messing the gravel—and look, everybody's taking pictures of you."

It was true. Thirty single-lens reflexes had pivoted from everywhere, proving that given a choice of recording a pretty girl with a man on his knees in front of her and a cast-iron mobile, the warm bodies will win every time.

Carson rose and dusted himself off, sighing, "What does it take? How long, oh Lord, how long!"

She smiled and said, "Put this stuff in the trash and come on. You guys are more trouble than you're worth."

11

CARSON WAS FURIOUS BEFORE HE HUNG UP the phone. He had called Dr. Robert Charter to ask for an appointment, and in the space of three paragraphs Charter had made it clear that almost anything he had to do was more important than talking to Carson. He expressed the thought that the affair was none of Carson's business and that the earliest he was likely to be able to work him in was after Israel petitioned to become a part of Egypt or the United States had joined Russia, whichever came first. Carson choked back a detailed exegesis of Charter's intelligence, morals, and relations with his mother, and said instead, "Well, I hate to have you feel that way, Dr. Charter. Mr. George's friend in the police department is due back tonight, and undoubtedly the first question he's going to ask us is, 'Who do you think did it?' My being the first to find the body keeps giving me a status I would be happy to avoid, but the fact is I'm afraid your own role is the most misunderstood—no, no, I should say, the least understood. It is grossly unfair that so many things should point to . . . well, that may not be fair either. It's just that I did want to have talked to you before I talk to . . . before Lieutenant Conrad gets back. It does seem only just to hear your side of the story . . ."

Charter at least had the grace to recede slowly. "Well, if it means so much to you, I guess I could give you fifteen minutes. If you'll wait for me in the faculty club, I'll try to get there between three and three thirty . . . or so. Do you know where the club is? Ah, but you're still in student status, aren't you? They won't let you in the building. We'll have to meet at the library. If you'll wait just inside the main entrance, I'll try to be there as soon after three as I can. The library is the large building behind Admin. Even the freshmen should have heard of it. I hope."

Carson replaced the receiver with delicate and gentle care, rose, and said, "May you fry in hot hell for eternity plus two days. You sanctimonious son-of-a . . . I am going to nail your ass to the wall should you be as innocent as Stephen of Cloyes." He headed for the campus with his jaws clenched.

At three thirty-one, Robert Charter came into the university library lobby. Carson had had a full hour to get himself under control. He's trying to steam me and I will not be had, he thought. He smiled broadly and said, "No problem. Coming on you so late and without an appointment, it's a wonder you could work me in at all. Appreciate it. Do you want to talk here or . . . ?"

"Yes, I have so little time there's no sense our wasting it walking around. What is it you think you want?"

"Right. Real fast. Did you know that Dr. Vandermann had been a journalist in the forties?"

"No, someone made some reference to that at the Tavern. I assumed he had always been a medieval specialist. If what you allude to is accurate, it explains a lot of things."

"Like . . . ?"

"Well, his essential incompetence. He was a dilettante, you know. Glib. A popularizer without the capacity to analyze—and without shame."

"Were his credentials questionable?"

"I hadn't heard so. No, he simply was no scholar."

"You mean no publications?"

"Many publications. Most of them worthless."

"How did he get them published?"

"I could never understand. He claimed he made an esoteric topic readable. I wouldn't have believed there were that many gullible editors. Never underestimate the superficiality of the American professional."

"How was he regarded on campus?"

"Very few recognized how mediocre he was."

"You mean they thought he was good? What did his students think of him?"

"His classes were mobbed. Medievalism apparently is 'in.' "

"Did you know of any reason why he might have been killed?"

"I hardly think your role sustains such a weighty question."

Carson drove his nails into his forearms behind his back, but laughed and said, "We understand you underwrote Merton's insurance scheme. Is that correct?"

"You understand wrong. Where did you hear that canard? Merton was an obsequious . . . repellent . . . specimen. I wouldn't have given him directions to . . . to . . . ." An appropriate denigration escaped him and he appeared more embarrassed than the occasion called for. "I . . . he . . . no. Not a dime."

"Did he resent your refusal? Did he ever threaten you?"

"No one threatens me. He would not have dared."

"Did he get any money from the Lehman woman?"

"It would not be appropriate for me to discuss Madame Lehman's affairs."

"But you do know."

"If I knew."

Carson sensed that the arrogance was slipping and he could not understand why. He picked up the tempo of his queries.

"Have you been in that coin club from the first?"

"No. Only the last three years."

"Had you been collecting before that?"

"Of course. My family has been in international shipping since the eighteenth century. My original collection was created by the Charter who founded the firm. In Providence."

"Rum or molasses? What kind of coins do you specialize in?"

"Crowns."

"What's a . . . ?"

"A crown is a kind of coin—the large, most aristocratic numismatic piece. A silver dollar is a crown. Every nation has a supreme coin as the top of its minted series. These are the crowns. I collect them from all countries."

"That must be very spectacular," Carson said and meant it. "How old do they run?"

"They could not be made until the silver of the Incas reached Europe. The first examples appear around 1500."

"Did the Romans have anything like them? Would Barrow have any?"

"Nothing even approaching them."

"Re Barrow. You were giving him the needle yesterday. Do his achievements bother you? He has done things in your field, has he not?"

"What do you mean 'done'? Done as in 'the can do the can't teach'?"

"No, no. I put that badly. Do you agree with his attitude in international affairs? That is your field, isn't it?"

"Barrow is a civil servant. They aren't paid to think. They are paid to be civil servants. So far as I can see, Barrow never did anything. He must have been a total success. He surely was a total failure. Even you can see that. A walking wreck of a man."

"Did that happen since he retired?"

"How can you tell when a civil servant retires? Is it geography? They simply do nothing in a different place?"

"You don't consider yourself a civil servant?"

"This university is privately funded."

"Right. I forgot. I thought Barrow was in charge of our embassy in London—chief of station. Isn't that so?"

"Yes, but you would scarcely call him an innovative envoy."

"Have you published?"

"Of course."

"Where?"

"I don't think I need to provide you with a bibliography."

"Did you know any of the regents here?"

"My family have been benefactors of this university for six generations."

"Ah, that explains the early tenure."

Charter appeared to be dumbfounded. Such gaucherie taxed his credulity. He squinted at Carson and said, "But I should not have been surprised. You are a product of a land grant school, aren't you?

Somewhere in the agrarian belt, of course." With which he simply pivoted on his heel and walked out the front door, leaving Carson grinning in place. Having no intention of pursuing him, Carson waited until Charter would have been well away and then left the building himself.

Not good, Carson thought to himself. Blurred a battle and lost a war. Learned nothing and snapped an avenue of intelligence. Clumsy.

But it *was* fun, he thought, and waved down a cab.

12

CRIGHTON CALLED ELEANOR YORK SHORTLY after noon. Eleanor appeared delighted to join Crighton for dinner and suggested that they make it themselves in Eleanor's apartment. Crighton picked Eleanor up at five thirty at Eleanor's Farragut Square office, by six thirty supper was prepared, by seven thirty it was eaten, and by eight they were sprawled at opposite ends of an enormous, modern couch, alternating between coffee and brandy.

"Ah," said Crighton, "what a delightfully sybaritic arrangement. You make me feel like I'm finally living as I so manifestly deserve. You have a beautiful apartment."

"Thank you, it serves," Eleanor replied.

Crighton looked at her, thinking of Carson's remark about "what a waste." Eleanor had changed into blue jeans so the long legs that Steve found so distracting were cased, but Crighton thought, I suspect he would find her just as attractive. She had a long, self-

96

possessed look about her, and he was right, it was her intelligence that made the difference. She was obviously as bright as she was beautiful.

"You know that fink Carson thinks you're the most beautiful woman he's ever seen, and I suspect he's right. Have you been married? How have you managed to keep your freedom for so long?"

"You just answered the question. Freedom," Eleanor replied. "I can think of nothing a man can give me that would compensate for the loss of it. I've never met one good enough to trade it in for."

"Are you into lib?" Crighton asked.

"Hardly. It's too much fun playing the woman and cutting them down to size. They think that by being chivalrous they're condescending to be good to us. I figure that by getting them chivalrous I can lead them any way I want. I wouldn't give that up for anything. Anyway, lib implies we're their equal. Hah! I consider myself their superior in every way." She laughed and traded a coffee cup for a brandy snifter.

"Steve acts like he wants to marry me. Should I?"

"I wouldn't even guess what's right for you. You're the only one who could possibly tell. It's all such a mix-up what really matters. What gives you kicks? What're you into that'll last for twenty years? I'd never marry a man for just a while. If I ever do it, it'll be for the long haul. That's why I'd be perfectly willing to live with some guy if he had anything to offer, but marriage . . . Not very likely with what I've seen so far. But that's me. Would you be better off with or without? You're the only one who would know. What matters to you?"

"Of course I *don't* know. If I did, I'd have done something about it long since. Do things ever get that clear?"

Eleanor laughed. "Never. I've got this bright gold balance scale in my mind labeled 'Satisfaction.' One pan is 'pain' and the other 'pleasure.' When I try to make a decision I load up the two pans and see which way it swings. The fool gimmick actually works most of the time. The problem is, of course, the times where you don't know which pan to put the fact in! But I just play it a day at a time and hope for the best."

"Do you worry about losing your looks?"

"Not for a minute. While I can make a few points on the body I'll use it. When it goes, I'd like to think I'll be able to take up the slack with faster footwork."

97

"Brainwork, you mean."

"Whatever."

"How did you get into the . . . what is it? . . . dental? . . . business?"

Eleanor's laugh ran a contralto scale that Crighton thought would have wiped Carson out completely. Why did she keep seeing her through Carson's eyes? she thought. A strange perspective.

"That's a wild sequence. I was strictly humanities at Trinity—Georgetown. That's when I got mixed up with this coin bunch. Then I got an afternoon job in a dentist's office to make money and I suddenly got such dates you wouldn't believe! I discovered there was a natural selection there that was out of this world. I'd lucked into a class operation, and the kind of men that turned up were rich and respectable—and young. I typed next to the receptionist and in the space of a month I'd filled up my calendar so it was all I could do to keep the classes going." She smiled with obvious pleasure at the memories. "I began to eat better immediately. I was going to places I'd never even seen except in magazines with guys I'd watched on television. Washington is big on action, you know. There's no question power appeals to me—I find it attractive—I don't want it myself. Anyway, the rest of the education went by very quickly. I was learning more off campus than on, so after the Georgetown degree I got the doctor to send me to the Polifax Labs in Boston for six months and I came out hell on wheels with the gadgetry and I'm really pretty good at the job—all things considered. The pay's not bad and it leaves me fresh for whatever turns up in the evenings."

Her eyes swept the room with earthy satisfaction. Crighton wondered how much the look implied.

"Hey!" Crighton said. "Have you got any of those coins around the place? They're all I've heard about for the past two days, but I still haven't seen one. Your specialty again was . . ."

"English hammered. Sure, I've got a handful in the other room. Come on. I'll show them to you."

She led Crighton into what the architect must have designed as a third bedroom, but which she was using as a study. Two of the walls were floor to ceiling books, and a large table with a modernistic elbow lamp over it stood in the center. The table was leather-topped, but Eleanor threw a green felt cloth across it and motioned Crighton to sit opposite her. She brought a small cabinet out of the closet and set it on the table by the lamp. It contained a half-dozen shallow drawers and she extracted one and selected a silver coin about the size of a quarter from among many, each resting in its own circular, felt-lined hole.

"Here's a Mary groat that'll show you what all the talk's about."

She handed it to Crighton, who took it gingerly. "Is it all right to touch it?"

"Sure. In fact rubbing helps to keep them clean. You never shine them. Finger handling is better to hit that sublime mixture of use and patina that's so big. Just don't drop it. After a few hundred years they get brittle and can crack in two if they fall the wrong way."

"A few hundred years, she says," said Crighton. "How old is this?"

"Well, Mary came before Elizabeth. That puts her around 1550."

"Oh, you meant Queen Mary! I thought you meant Mary the . . . Virgin Mary."

"No, no. This is Bloody Mary. Instant martyrs."

Crighton looked more intently and saw a portrait of a delicate, very feminine young woman with flowing hair and wearing a small graceful crown.

"She doesn't look so tough."

"No, I always pictured her as the Wicked Witch of the West myself. The coins of Elizabeth and Henry the Eighth look just like their pictures. If Mary's is as accurate as theirs, that must have been the way she looked." She retrieved the coin and selected two more and handed them to Crighton.

"How come you've got these at home?" Crighton asked. "Don't you keep yours in a bank like we were told?"

"Oh, yes. Mine are in a safe deposit drawer just like everybody else's. These are just new ones I've gotten since I made the last trip. Safe deposit things are a pain. They're only open during the day and I never seem to be loose when they are."

"Can you insure coins?" Crighton asked, remembering Carson's suggestion.

"Not practically. The companies won't pay more than five hundred dollars on household accounts, and thereafter the premiums run two dollars a hundred so the insurance would eat up the profits. It's cheaper to keep 'em in the bank—but more inconvenient."

"Then those ones that were stolen were total losses?"

"After five hundred, I suspect yes."

"Why 'hammered'? Are they really?"

"They really are. You see how the coins are all sort of thin and a little irregular around the edges? That's the way they're made. In medieval times they would take a hunk of silver, pound it out thin, cut a little circle the size they wanted, trim it to the proper weight, and then put the circle on an anvil. They'd have carved the design of the coin in the anvil and they set the blank on the design. Then they'd take another piece of iron with the back design carved in it, put it on the blank, and literally take a sledgehammer and slam it down. The two designs would be mashed into the coin and you'd have the 'hammered coinage,' literally made by hand, so no two were exactly alike. This is the way they did it from the Dark Ages up to about 1650—Cromwell, in English coins—when the French invented a machine and they've been milled ever since. Took all the fun out of it."

"But these portraits are incredibly delicate. You can see every pearl and the eyelids and hair. You say they were slammed on an anvil?"

"That's it. They became marvelously skilled at it. There are pieces of the first Elizabeth sitting on a horse that are more detailed than anything we make now."

"So we have a pretty good idea what the kings and queens really looked like. I didn't realize that. How far back do they go?"

"Not too. The first one to put his face on it was Henry the Seventh, father of the Eighth. Before then, you had generalized portraits of a male head with a crown. Here's a beautiful one. It's a groat of Henry the Fifth."

"Is that Shakespeare's Henry Fifth? 'Oh, for a muse of fire?' "

"That's the lad."

"It's beautiful."

"I agree. So did the medieval kings, incidentally. They used that design from Edward up to Henry Seven—two hundred years. They just changed their name around the edge and the mint marks. You see it says Henric and that thing on the back"—she turned the coin over and pointed to a design at the top—"is a mint mark—a flared cross in this case." She pulled out another drawer and selected a coin that looked exactly like the one Crighton was holding, but Eleanor said, "You see, this says Ricard and the mint mark is a boar's head." Crighton looked at it, and it did indeed look like the silhouette of a boar's head on a banner.

"How much are these worth?" Crighton asked, holding the two coins, one in each hand.

"Oh, the Henry Five is good for about two hundred and fifty dollars. The Richard Three is nearly a thousand."

"Yikes! And you just leave them around?"

"Well, they're in the cabinet. They're not going anywhere on their own, and I'm reasonably trustworthy." She laughed.

"Are these scarce? Do you know how many of them exist?"

"As a matter of fact, both of them are rare. We only have a general sense of how many there are—it's just a feel the trade gets from how often people offer them for sale. But, oddly enough, we know very precisely on some of the very old coins and for a strange reason." She returned the various coins she had been handling to the cabinet and pulled out another drawer with smaller ones in it.

"These are silver pennies," she said. "They're the only coins there were in Europe from the time the Romans split until Edward I invented that groat you had. Every one of these had a different design and the backs have the names of the guys who slammed 'em." She handed Crighton a shiny one about the size of a dime. "That was struck for William the Conqueror at Dorchester by a guy named Godric. See? His name is stamped around the back circle."

By tilting it toward the light a couple of times, Crighton made out the lettering rather easily.

"That's what's called a PAXS penny, and it was the rarest of all the William the Conqueror designs. There were only four known in the world. Two in the British Museum, one in a museum in York, and one on the Isle of Man. Then, just before Victoria arrived, a farmer down in Hampshire was digging a ditch to put in some drainage tile and he hit a lead box containing over six thousand of 'em! Now they're the commonest William there is—and one of the commonest of all hammered coins."

"Worth . . ."

"Oh, a couple hundred dollars. Henry the Second—*The Lion in Winter* type—issued a new design that was fairly rare—maybe a hundred or so left in the world, and then they found a hoard that apparently had been buried under the floor of a manor house at Tealby in Lincolnshire. That hoard had over five thousand coins in

101

it, so the locals took it to the authorities, who saved a handful and melted down forty-five hundred of them to get the silver—in modern times, yet! Can you believe it? The result is Tealbies are still very scarce and a good one will bring four or five hundred dollars. Most of 'em are in lousy condition too. Henry was striking them in the field to pay off his soldiers and they look it."

"How often does this sort of thing happen? Finding them today . . ."

"Nothing on the scale of the Beaworth or Tealby has hit us recently, but we're still getting ten or a dozen new finds every year—everything from a half-dozen coins to several hundred. Last year a telephone company was trenching for a cable in Denmark, of all places, and they hit a leather bag of two hundred Canutes that had been struck in England around 1000. Some Viking had ripped off some Danegeld, apparently. I had six of the coins before the find, and I had heart failure the market was going to drop out on them." She laughed. "But the find got so much publicity that even our originals went up."

"What would one of these buy when they were new?"

"A penny was supposed to be the price of an ox. The records show a penny was a year's taxes on a manor or would buy a hogshead of wine or twelve sheep—then inflation set in and it's never stopped. See that cross on the back? It was perfectly permissible to cut the coin in half along the arms of the cross and get two ha'pennies—halfpennies—which were worth the equivalent of ten dollars. A pair of shoes or a week's pay for a carpenter. If you cut it along both arms of the cross, you have four-fourths of a penny—farthings. That was the only change they had. It's funny, cut coins were far more common than whole ones, but when a king would bring out a new coin—as they did every so often, the cut coins would be brought in to be melted down and traded for new coins, so the cut pieces are almost nonexistent today, but the whole ones, of course, are still around for us to mess with."

At which point the doorbell rang.

Eleanor looked up with a puzzled expression and said, "Excuse me. That's the door."

Crighton made herself comfortable, and she could soon hear a man's voice at the end of the hall, when a second bell rang in the room beside her and she realized it was an extension phone sitting in the bookcase.

"Will you get that, please?" Eleanor shouted. "Take the number!"

Crighton answered it, found it to be a woman who accepted the delay without comment and gave her name and number with a cheerful, "Any time. Tomorrow would be fine." She hung up, leaving Crighton with two pieces of information and no place to record them. Crighton hurriedly looked around the room, found nothing, lifted the green felt cover on the table and tried the drawer below, where to her relief she discovered paper and a ball-point before the data escaped her. She recorded it and was on the point of closing the drawer again when she realized she was looking at five medieval coins lying loose among the clutter in the desk. She picked one up and tilted it toward the light with the realization that it was another of the large coins she had just seen with the head of a king. Not the portrait, she thought, the other one. The Shakespearean one. She turned over the one she held and saw the boar's head silhouette even more clearly than on the one she had been shown earlier. Now, working quickly and somewhat guiltily, she looked at the other four and was further surprised to find them apparently exactly alike, each with the same design and each with a boar's head stamped on the back. She replaced them all, shoved the drawer shut, and let the green felt cover fall back as before.

She laid the paper with the name and phone number on the shelf beside the phone itself and then walked toward the door to see if Eleanor might have seen her going through the furniture. Eleanor was still at the front door at the extreme opposite end of the apartment, talking through a six-inch crack. Whoever had called had not been invited in. Indeed, now that she was concentrating on the scene, Crighton could hear Eleanor's low voice saying, "No. Not now. This is the worst possible time. Look, I'll call you tomorrow."

Apparently to emphasize her refusal, she shook her head firmly, and opened the door just wide enough for Crighton to see an indignant Robert Charter starting to step inside. Eleanor shoved the door in his face, closing it, and Crighton jumped back into the study and hastily returned to her seat at the table.

Eleanor returned shaking her head.

"Irritating," she said. "That was the fool paper boy claiming I hadn't paid him for the month. I know perfectly well . . . who was on the phone?"

"I put it over there."

"Fine. I'll get it later. Where were we?"

"Uh," Crighton grabbed the first thing that came into her mind and asked, "Uh, where do you buy the coins?"

"All over. The British send out catalogs, and you trade with people you meet at the conventions. The big houses like Spink's and Baldwin's in England and Sotheby Parke Bernet here all have estate auctions. I like auctions best, I guess. They appeal to my competitive spirit. They send out lists of coins with descriptions— even pictures of the best ones—and then you send in and tell them you'll pay up to blah, then the house bids for you at the sale and ultimately you either get a 'sorry' letter or the coin itself with a bill. Adds excitement to my otherwise drab existence. Of course I buy a lot out of catalogs from Seaby's in London just like you buy stamps from Macy's. Come on, let's go back in and reheat the coffee."

The two women returned to the living room and Crighton dropped back on the couch as Eleanor went into the kitchen.

"Just half a cup for me," Crighton shouted after her. "I'm supposed to pick up Steve and Mr. George. This has been great."

Eleanor returned with the cups and eased onto the couch again.

"How are you going to play the Carson thing, do you think?" she asked.

"I waver. The answer depends on what hour you ask." Crighton laughed.

"Don't let him rush you. I don't know how the idea that women are the romantics got started. My experience is that there's nothing as romantic as a man. I mean the . . . fantasizing . . . making fairy princesses. Most of 'em are totally out of touch with reality. They make up this technicolored world we're supposed to live in for them, and they're absolutely astonished when we don't play the role. Don't hurry into anything. I'm convinced living with a man can be mighty seedy—and boring—and you're a long time sorry."

Crighton's mind jumped to Carson's picture of Eleanor. What a shock it would be to him to hear her now. And she suspected he'd say, "What a waste."

"Thank you so much for a fascinating evening, " Crighton said. "I'd best split or I'll leave those two innocents standing on a dark sidewalk. If you'll point me to my coat I'll be gone."

And shortly she was—as it happened—straight to the police.

13

WHEN EDWARD GEORGE HAD TELEPHONED
Lieutenant Conrad of the D.C. police the Sunday morning after the
first murder, he had been told that Conrad was away from his office
for a week and would not return until Monday night. The
communications officer had, however, passed George on to Conrad's
assistant, a Sergeant Jesse. And Jesse had been most cordial. The
cordiality revealed that, one, Conrad had gone to Chicago for a one-
week course on lie detection equipment. Two, he had intended to
drive back to Washington, slowly, by way of southern Canada, to
see the fall colors. Three, he was not due into work until Tuesday
morning; but four, the sergeant would be astonished if he did not
turn up Monday on the way to his house, and where could he reach
George? George had provided the necessary information and let
Jesse in on their present problem in the hope that Conrad might
look into it before he returned the call. They had parted at that
point, and George was therefore pleased if not too surprised to find

105

that Conrad had called while he was returning from his visit with Barrow at Gadsby's Tavern.

Crighton, with Eleanor York's words still in her ears, had pushed the speed limit for all of its posted-plus-five percent down the Mall, and arrived at the Werner-Bok only seconds late. The two men were waiting on the sidewalk, and as they climbed into the Audi, George said, "Our old friend Conrad is back at his post, and insists we come straight over tonight. Is it possible you two are free for another hour and we could wander toward the police department? I'm eager to see if they know anything we don't."

"Great," she said. "We're both available, and I'll feel much more comfortable having the calm hand of the law beside us."

"They don't come much calmer than Comrade Conrad," Carson said. "One part sardonic mixed with two parts taciturn."

George smiled in recollection. "I think we can drink to that. What kind of day did you two have?"

There followed a furious exchange of information while each brought the others up to date on the day's interviews. The debriefing had barely finished when Crighton drove into a parking lot beside the District Building. George said, "Bless your hearts, I am simply delighted. A very profitable afternoon. We collected more data in less time than I would have thought possible. Let us find out what Conrad knows and then see if we can fit it all together. I wonder how he's held up these past six months."

Lieutenant Conrad was a gray, heavyset man who had a technique of talking just one decibel above a whisper. This automatically got everybody's attention and shut up dialogues as far as the ear could hear. His perpetual understatement was more a disgusted cynicism than a philosophical comment. Given his reluctance to show any kind of emotion, the smile and firm handshakes he gave the group would have amounted to screaming, yelling, and distribution of alcohol in any other situation. Old Home Week at Leavenworth, Carson thought.

"Come in and sit down," Conrad said, pointing to various steel chairs around his desk. "Wait a minute. Let me shut the door."

They settled themselves in the new silence.

"You've got yourselves into another one, I see," Conrad said.

"Yes, we backed into this one," George replied. "And believe me, as soon as we can work off some obligations, we will leave it firmly

106

in your hands. Have you had a chance to look into it at all?"

"Yeah, I got the file out and I talked to a couple of people. Weird one."

"Do you have a suspect yet?"

"Hardly. It only happened this morning. They've spent the whole day running the routine. How long have you been messing with it?"

"Couple of days."

"You know this guy Merton?"

"Ah," said George. "Where to start? I don't think this is the time to go into much detail—you've got to get home, and there's plenty of time for that tomorrow, but in a nutshell, do you know about the murder of a Professor Vandermann Saturday night in Virginia? Down near Mount Vernon?"

"Fairfax County," said Carson.

"Yeah, that's referred to here, but there's no details. I understand they talked to them down there on the phone and they're going out to see 'em tomorrow. What's that got to do with this Merton one?"

"All right. This is the situation. This man Vandermann started a club about ten years ago made up of coin collectors—you know, old coins—and not American. Anything we've done would be considered beneath the dignity of this group. They're interested in foreign gold and silver.

"Anyway, this Vandermann was both the founder and the president of the club, and he'd discovered that one of his so-called Executive Committee was going to kill him, or so he believed. He was on the verge of telling Steve and me what he knew about this threat when we visited his house and found him shot dead at his desk. In addition to the body, there was valuable house silver and old coins spread around, apparently about to be taken away. The Fairfax police think we had stumbled into a burglary. We think the appearance of a burglary was a screen to cover a well-planned murder.

"We then set out to talk with everyone involved in the Executive Committee and by last night we'd gotten enough information together to point—at least in my opinion—to one of the group: Merton. I was on the verge of taking some kind of action when he too was found dead. If you're interested, I'll explain the steps involved in my conclusion tomorrow. What's important now is, Steve and I think we actually saw the person who killed Vandermann, and presumably it was the same person who killed Merton. When you looked over the file, did you get any hint of a likely target?"

"No, here it all is." Conrad patted a rather thin manila folder. "They spent the day taking pictures and interviewing all over that apartment house. No one saw anyone go into the room or go up the elevator or heard a shot—and so on. Nothing. But it took all day. Someone gave 'em the names of this coin club bunch too, but nobody's got to them yet either."

"Ummm. When do they think the murder was committed?" George asked.

Conrad consulted the file. "Between ten and midnight."

"And no one heard anything."

"No."

"I understand the door was ajar when someone walked in this morning. Were the lights on?"

"Yeah."

"And the night latch?"

"Yeah. The guy must have let the murderer in himself. There's no evidence of anything being forced—or this bird Merton being surprised. Nothing messed up or pushed around."

"We heard he was handcuffed to a chair."

"Right."

"Vandermann was too, and we found news stories of other robberies around the area where the same thing occurred. Would you be sure that someone compares the handcuffs on Merton with those on Vandermann? Also try to find out where they were purchased."

"They're already working on the where did they come from. I'll have 'em see how they match with the . . . other ones." He made a note to himself with great deliberation.

"You should compare the wounds or caliber or whatever too. It would be useful to know if they were both made by the same gun."

"Yeah." He wrote again.

"Was there anything in the apartment that was odd—beside the handcuffs? Any note or writing or anything?" George asked.

"No, just the coin in the man's hand."

"Coin? What coin?"

All three of them leaned toward the lieutenant.

Conrad leafed through more sheets of the reports and then read,

" 'One old, thin, silver coin was held in the closed fist of the victim's right hand.' According to the Polaroids, his left hand was on the table and his right hand was hanging down at his side."

"Were there other coins on the table or any place around?"

"No. This was the only one outside of the change in his pocket."

George turned toward the young people. "I wonder if the murderer cleaned the place out and took it with him or there was nothing to be taken?"

"I'll bet something was there," Carson said. "All these guys seemed to have some of the things around, and Merton must have been handling some to have one in his hand."

"I wonder what kind of a coin it was. What was Merton's specialty?"

"Queen Victoria," Crighton said. "Heads, according to Dr. Vandermann."

"That's right," Carson agreed.

"Where is that coin now?" George asked.

"Lemme think. The body'll be at a mortuary—no, it may still be at the morgue, but I doubt it. Anyway, the contents of the pockets should be out front. Lemme see."

He made three calls and in a very short time a uniformed woman came through the door and handed him a large, thick envelope. Conrad opened the clasp and very carefully let the contents spill out onto his blotter. He found a ruler in his desk drawer and, using it as a pusher, shoved the billfold and handkerchief aside revealing a number of coins—two quarters, several nickels and dimes, and one piece of hammered coinage that brought Crighton to her feet in one swift movement. She leaned over the blotter.

"Oh, no! Can you turn it over?"

"I think all this stuff has been dusted for prints, but you can't be sure. Wait a minute." Conrad slipped a piece of paper under the coin and turned it on its face. Crighton moved her head back and forth until the light was reflected at the angle she wanted.

"That's it!" she said. "There's no question. That is a boar's head groat—exactly like those in the drawer. That makes . . . seven of them. One in the fancy tray, five in the drawer, and this. And they're supposed to be so rare they're worth a thousand dollars apiece."

"Jesus," said Carson. "Now what the hell does that mean?"

George hastily recounted what they knew about the coin to

Conrad and then said slowly, "Children, I think we must find out precisely what coins were stolen from those sixteen collections. You will recall that of all the kinds of coins people seem to collect, the computer carries every one of the stolen ones as 'English.' English what? Do you suppose it could have been English hammered? And . . ." His voice went silent as his speculations began to build. "No, not now," he said. "Is there anything else out of the ordinary that might be of help? The car? Who was where? Alibis?"

Conrad shook his head. "All that's just started. They'll know more tomorrow. I hope."

"Then let's not detain you any longer now. Lieutenant, I can't tell you how much we appreciate this. You have been much too kind. Let me call you tomorrow and I'll come over and give you the details on what we know. I have not forgotten your instruction to me the last time. 'There's nothing that can't be explained by money, booze, or sex.' I am looking. Just as you told me."

Conrad said nothing, but his broad smile expressed satisfaction— unusual for him. They said their good-byes, and the three went quickly to Crighton's Audi.

George asked, "Is there a McDonald's around here? I think we need a staff meeting."

"There's one up on Capitol Hill, just behind the Library of Congress. Five minutes at the most—provided we can find a place to park. Want to try it?"

It took fifteen, but they were soon crowded into a booth in the back of the Ronald Room (i.e., cellar).

"All right, troops," said George, "we're down to the last few hours of our allotted time. Conservation of energy. What are our unknowns?"

"Those weird groats," Crighton answered. "How come so many? Why so casually thrown loose in that drawer? What did the one in Merton's hand mean?"

"Good. Let's start with that. What explanations do we have to choose from?"

Carson looked at the ceiling and said slowly, "One. Nothing odd about York's. She's simply specializing in them. Not viable. Possibility of damaging five thousand dollars' worth of coins keeps them from being thrown loose anywhere. Why loose? Because they aren't worth a thousand dollars each. Why not? One, she was lying

110

to Crite about their value. Not likely. Two, because they're counterfeit? I like that. How do you tell counterfeit coins? How do you make them? Who makes them? What if you get caught? Who does what to whom?"

"Very good," George said. "That's the first thing we've got to look into tomorrow. Counterfeits. Fakes and forgeries. Steve, do you want to take that on? Stored data. Flat research."

"Good. Do you have any of your old librarian's tricks? Forgive me. Shortcuts."

George laughed. "No. I'd suggest two routes. If I were you I'd start with the traditional books and then wander on to the computer. Just watch your subject headings."

"Watch? What're they doing?"

"Frustrating you, probably. The curse of our card catalogs is that we don't have time to analyze books anymore. My generation did all kinds of efficiency studies and decided we couldn't afford to give any book more than two headings. When you read a hundred-thousand-word volume and have to tell what's in it with only two terms, your only hope is to use the most precise ones you've got. As I recall, in this area you've got something like three choices: Forgery, or Art Forgeries, or Counterfeiting. And that is it. Period."

"So? Why mention it? You're about to slip me another one of your 'I suppose you thought but the real truth is . . . ,' aren't you?"

George laughed again. "Well, just think what you're missing. Suppose you want famous *painting* forgeries. We wouldn't even mention the book under Paintings even if the book is full of paintings. It would go solely under Art Forgeries or whatever. Suppose you want famous coin forgeries. You won't find it among the cards on Coins. Just under Counterfeiting . . . You have to outguess us librarians, or the book is completely lost to you. You always have to go *up* the vocabulary from the very specific to the general. We stop with the bottom rung."

"I hope I'm misunderstanding you."

"No, you're not. Take your own subject. Suppose you want to know what a library has about pioneers. You look up Pioneers and find five books. You think you've got them all. But if there's a book about pioneers in Illinois it won't be mentioned at all under Pioneers. It goes under Illinois history. Nothing under Pioneers. But if it's about early pioneers in Chicago, you can't find it under

111

Pioneers *or* Illinois. It goes under Chicago history. Always the smallest, most precise heading. Early pioneers at Fort Dearborn? Doesn't appear under Pioneers *or* Illinois *or* Chicago. Just Fort Dearborn, the beginning of Chicago."

"Jesus H. Christ. You mean the user has to guess where all the books could be?"

"That's the problem. We try to give you some hints among the see-also cards, but they won't represent one lead in ten. That's one of the tricks of having all card catalogs made of the same kind of furniture. They look so organized, we intimidate the user. 'They must know what they're doing . . . I must be doing it wrong.'" George laughed wryly. "That's why we embraced the computer so eagerly. We thought we could dump dozens of headings onto every book we cataloged so when we analyzed a book it would appear in dozens of places where people would be looking."

Crighton said defensively, "So what's the matter with that?"

"Well, there have proved to be a few problems: someone has to type all those dozens of subject headings in—'input them'—and this costs umpteen dollars an hour. Too many headings and the storage gets full and you have to buy another trillion-dollar computer. Too many headings and you paralyze the user—what have you gained if you ask for pioneers and we tell you the names and numbers of the five thousand books about early settlers in the fifty states one book at a time? Everything has cost more and taken longer . . . et cetera, et cetera, et cetera. Not to mention the fact that the computer is dead half the time."

Carson said, "I'm punchy."

"Then forget everything I just said and remember to look under Counterfeits or Counterfeiting and you'll probably learn more than you wanted to know anyway. Then when you've read the few books we grudgingly tell you about, you can go over to the computer and see if there have been any recent examples . . . news stories . . . about forgeries in our time—like since Christmas."

Carson buried his face in his hands and George said, "Any other angles on the groats?"

"I wish we could compare the seven," Crighton said. "Since all these coins are made by hand, and the two anvils or whatever are held at different angles and stuff, individual ones can't be identical. The fronts and backs must be twisted differently and even slid across different. It would be interesting to see how much variety there is in the group. And you're so right, I wonder too if there were any boar's heads among those sixteen thefts."

"That's the second unknown," George said. "Tomorrow we must visit some of these victims and see what they lost. Do you have the names, Steve?"

"Not with me, but I've got 'em. I'll bring them in tomorrow. I got the addresses on all of them and I tried 'em against the city directories, but there was no pattern apparent. I thought maybe all the victims might be ex-foreign service or retired military or some unity but there was nothing I could see other than that most of them were middle-aged or elderly—which probably means you can't afford that kind of investment until you have discretionary income."

" 'Discretionary income?' Where have I heard that phrase . . . ?" George asked. "Madame Lehman. She said Barrow's discretionary income could never have exceeded five thousand dollars a year."

"There's another unknown," Crighton said. "Where has all this money come from? We're talking about massive chunks of cash in this bunch. Is it simply chance, or is there some single source of capital running here?"

"Well, what options have we got on that one?" Carson replied. "They could be passing black market money around from their European adventures. That would account for Vandermann, Barrow, and Lehman—but Merton and York don't seem to have any ties there, and probably not Charter either."

"Forgive my even thinking of it, but York might have made it sleeping around—on pretty high-priced furniture," said Crighton.

"Jones!" Carson shouted. "What a thing to say about that innocent beauty. Clearly the sole support of an aged mother. Walks on green lights, never steps on baby chicks . . ."

"Hah!" she replied. "There is a hard-bitten wench if I've ever seen one. And there's another unknown. What was she doing playing footsie with Brother Charter in the middle of the night?"

"You mean, why was my great and good friend Professor Charter, scion of one of New England's oldest and finest families, visiting this attractive and charming young lady at a perfectly respectable nine o'clock in the evening? How you wrong the both of them!"

"I noticed you nearly choked trying to get that out. Sufficient unto the nonsense is the evil . . ."

They laughed and Carson said, "Let's go back to the big ones. We

113

still don't know why Vandermann and Merton had to be killed. We mustn't forget that this implies something pretty massive. There's no casual pique here."

George replied seriously, "Very well taken, and note something else. Vandermann was killed Saturday night, Merton was killed Sunday night. We are now at Monday night. Not only must we be very careful ourselves, should we have reminded anyone of this? Conrad? The participants?"

"There's a telling bit," Carson said. "I can see you calling Madame Lehman, and I can see Crite calling York, but I haven't the faintest desire to protect Brother Charter and we keep forgetting Barrow. Is there any truth to be learned from that?"

"I don't know what it would be," George said, "short of a popularity contest . . . No, I don't think it points up vulnerability . . . or just desserts. What are you getting at? That we might have a 'feel' for who deserves it or something?"

"No, I don't know what I had in mind. It was just a random thought."

"And I'm not sure it was accurate to begin with," Crighton said. "If you'd asked me cold, I'd have said Mr. George or someone should have called Madame Lehman, but I have no particular feeling of protection for Eleanor. I don't *not* want her protected, but there is a very real feeling about her that she can protect herself all by herself. Charter seems so glacial no one would dare threaten him. Barrow's the pitiful one. I think I'd have called him first and warned him. He's really vulnerable."

"Probably true," Carson said.

"I think we're spinning our wheels. Stirring clear water in a pail," George said. "It's probably fatigue and we might as well call it a night. I have just two queries that are haunting me. Have we really asked the classic questions? Who had the opportunity? Who had the motive? Let's try the first. Who could have killed Vandermann?"

"You said Madame Lehman convinced you everyone could have or anyone," Crighton said.

"All right. She claimed Barrow was at an unprovable movie, Merton was driving around alone—where was Charter?"

"With a woman," Carson said.

"That sounds the least likely," Crighton remarked.

George smiled. "And Lehman and York were supposed to be

together. Do we have any reason to think they were really covering for each other? I would think not. Do either of you sense an alliance there?"

"Just the opposite," Crighton said. "At least York is flat out scared of Lehman."

"And Lehman expresses a distaste for York," George said. "So opportunity makes Merton, Barrow, and Charter the prime candidates for having killed Vandermann."

"Come on, scratch Charter," Carson said. "He wouldn't dare fake a date. She'd be too easy to break down."

"Maybe," George said. "All right. If we solve it by opportunity, only Merton or Barrow could have killed Vandermann."

"And who had the opportunity to kill Merton?" Crighton asked.

"We've got to wait for Conrad on that, but the field is narrowing the hard way. The only ones still with us are Charter, Lehman, York, and Barrow. And my brain is getting tired. Let's move that one over to tomorrow's unknowns. So finally, Conrad's Law: he claims he never saw a murder that couldn't be explained by money, booze, or sex. Does that do us any good?"

Carson said, "We ought to be able to knock off booze pretty easily. Surely the flinty Madame Lehman never dulls her cutting edge. Crite? The lovely Leah?"

Crighton stuck out her tongue at him and said, "Nope. Not in my presence. Moderation in all things."

"I saw Barrow drink two-thirds of a tankard of beer in one draft, but I'd be surprised if you could generalize it into anything. Charter no, Merton unknown. Drink is not obvious. Money?"

"We don't know enough about that either," Carson said. "Is the family firm threatened for Charter? The police could find out easier than we could. York . . . ?"

"As long as she's got her figure she's in good shape," Crighton said.

"Woman, you are hateful. But I agree. She seems to be living on top of the world. Lehman? Everybody says she's rich as Croesus and boy, does she look it. Barrow? They say he's rich too, but he doesn't look it at all. Cops again. You might suggest to Conrad he run their various bank accounts. Merton we knew was starving. You think he stole to get it the first time, Mr. George. Why did 'X' knock him off? To get the money? Who needed it worse than Merton?"

"Another variable, and we'll sic Conrad on it. And sex?

Crighton's friend Eleanor has attracted Barrow and Merton and Charter that we know of. Madame Lehman attracted Vandermann in their early days. I'm rather inclined to think these linkages and the resultant rejections and jealousies—emotional irrationalities for a bunch of very cerebral, rational people—may be where the pay dirt lies. Let's work on it. Put yourself in each of their places and try to guess how you'd feel—and what frustration would do. How would you resolve it . . . relieve it . . . revenge it . . . in each case? But not now." George straightened up somewhat painfully and slid out of the booth. "It's time to close down for the day. The past twelve hours have been very profitable. I think we have proceeded with efficiency."

"Are you going to let Conrad take over now, Mr. George?" Crighton asked.

"Heavens no," he answered. "He and the police might solve it eventually, but not near soon enough to do us any good. I am just as eager to clear . . . free up . . . our minds as I ever was. Steve is not going to be efficient until this is resolved, nor will I be. I won't be able to do anything original until I'm cleansed of this. No, I asked for forty-eight hours of your time and I have until tomorrow noon. I intend to have this finished by then."

"You're kidding!" Carson said. "Do you know how it all ties together?"

"No. In candor, I am further from a logical explanation than at any time since we began, but I have no intention of being intimidated by that. We have so much more information. Our chances of a logical resolution have increased enormously. All it takes is a little original thought now. The elements are here. What do they mean? How do they link together? Can you be my guests at the club for breakfast? Eight o'clock?"

"Fine by me," Crighton said. "Can I pick you up?"

"Hell yes!" Carson said. "Mr. George, I am as much in awe of your confidence as I am of your intellect. A team that won't be beaten can't be beaten! Or is it that can't be beaten . . . ? In any event, Crighton Jones, will you marry me? No, by God, we think positively around here. Crighton Jones, you are *going* to marry me. You are *going* to marry me. You are *going* to . . ."

Leitmotiv into the night.

116

14

I CAME ON THIS REPORT OF A U.S. CONSUL TO
Italy named Jerome. Early 1900s," Carson was saying.

It was eight o'clock Tuesday morning. The last day. George had
given himself until noon to do it, and the three were at breakfast at
the Minerva Club.

"He collected a mess of eyewitnesses who had actually seen the
eruption of Vesuvius from the town across the bay. Every one of
them had been standing in the same street, and they were all
looking in the same direction at the same time when the top blew
off the mountain—and the difference between what they all saw
boggles the mind. Jerome was using the incident to challenge Pliny
the Younger's description of the Pompeii disaster, but it's just as
applicable to our own situation. For what it's worth, Jerome was
trying to prove that just because Pliny was an eyewitness, one, it
didn't mean much to begin with, and two, since Pliny wrote it down
twenty-five or thirty years after the event, it meant even less to

117

history. Practically everything we've ever read about the destruction of Pompeii is based on Pliny's letters."

George said, "But at least the robbery victims have no concerted story to sell. What's making me so uncomfortable about the Executive Committee is that I have the sense they're all leading us around by the nose. It should be refreshing to hear someone who's simply telling it like it was, not like it ought to have been—from the Committee's varied points of view! At least we'll have first-person, primary sources."

Carson sighed. "Primary sources. I used to be very big on primary sources—until I got into this rhubarb with the trade. I set out to make an impassioned defense of the idea, but by the time I'd assembled all my evidence, I'd lost my own confidence in the concept! Pliny is one thing. Bancroft is quite another."

"Because . . . ?" Crighton asked.

"Well, you know all those psychology experiments where ten people are supposed to witness a staged crime and then every one of them sees it differently? The damn thing happens all the time. Everywhere."

"I have to agree," George said sadly. "Robin Winks back at Yale makes the marvelous point that we can't be accurate even if we want to be. He claims we're all members of minorities and we see everything that happens to us or around us as aspects of this. It's obvious if you're a black from Mississippi or a WASP in Israel, but he says it's just as real if you're a college graduate pumping gas or a high-school graduate at an Aspen conference. Your accent, your religion, your family relationship—are you involved in the event as a son, as a father, an in-law, a divorcée—makes you see and select and remember differently."

Crighton said, "That's all very fancy, but our problem here is simply: someone is lying. Never mind the perception bit."

"Fair enough." George laughed. "And that sounds like Winks too. He used to quote, 'A lie is a lie even if it's in Latin.' All right. How do we set the day? We're trying to find out what was taken in those sixteen robberies. How much of it can we get on the phone and how much do we have to do in person?"

"Some of the people may have nothing to do with our stuff at all," Crighton said. "Let's weed those out by calls and then visit the rest."

"Good, and there's no reason we can't start those at once—from here at the club. What time is it? Eight fifteen? Most people will be up and we can act like we're calling early to catch them before they leave for work—which we are. Let me get some change from the bursar, and there's a bank of pay phones in the cloakroom. Steve, have you got the names?"

"With numbers."

George left and Carson said, "Woman, you look good enough to eat this morning. Are you always so succulent at breakfast? How attractive you are to me, Crighton Jones. The hair. The eyes. Have I ever told you you have the sexiest pair of ears in . . ."

Crighton laughed and shook her head. "Doctor," she said, "he is very odd. Half the time he's threatening to consume me, and the rest he's working out his neuroses. You don't have an ear fetish, do you?"

"Terribly. Only it's highly specialized. It's not ears in general, it is Crighton Jones's ears. Very limited field. Makes treatment much more difficult. Now if I might suggest . . ."

She sighed. "Carson, what a nut you are—and so early in the morning. You know, Eleanor York is right. You men *are* all romantics. How do you get this way? It can't be cultural, it must be in the genes. Still . . . was your mother ever frightened by a Viennese operetta? Did you have a mother? Is it possible . . . ?"

George returned and said, "Come on, you two. To the phones."

He led them toward the front entrance of the club and turned into the cloakroom.

"There was a potential sixteen," he said. "Did you find them all?"

"I got all the names and addresses," Carson said, "but three involved deaths and we may not want to distress the families unless we have to. One has dropped out of the phone book."

"Twelve. That's still plenty for our purposes. Let's each take four and see what happens."

Fifteen minutes later they were back at the breakfast table picking up their second cups of coffee.

"All right, how did you do? Lady first."

"Three of my four answered," said Crighton. "The first guy collected English coins all right, but they were all copper and from the 1780s only. Get this, it's wild. You outlanders should know that our nearest Atlantic beach is Rehoboth, Delaware. We all stream over by the thousands on weekends."

"They come down from Baltimore too," Carson said. "Their

119

women are infinitely better. Lots of dark Italians and blond Germans. They . . ."

"Turkey!" Crighton shouted. "Will you . . . as I was saying before I was so rudely, it seems that in 1785 a ship carrying a bunch of Irish immigrants sank off Rehoboth, and ever since then big, fat English pennies have been washing up on the shore. They've even got a strip of sand that is known as Coin Beach, and after every storm all the local citizens rush down and pace back and forth looking for the things. It seems that the local high-school principal is the specialist and this guy I talked to has been buying these coins off him for twenty years. Here comes the kicker: all the coins are George III pennies from around 1780, but over half of them are counterfeits! No one knows why, but they've been recognized as such since the Civil War at least. The state museum at Lewes has a huge collection of them."

Carson said, "I'm sorry I asked. In fact, I didn't. Then how did we get stuck with all that trivia?"

"Because the computer said the stolen coins were English."

Carson held the top of his head, and George laughed and said, "Moving right along . . . "

"Yeah," Crighton continued. "My second call was to a guy named Wright, all his coins were stolen, they were all English hammered, and he has a list of every one. I told him we'd be out. Call three wasn't home, and call four specialized in the four Georges."

"One good hit, then," George said.

"Right."

"Steve?"

"My first specialized in George V colonials—modern coins with the head of George V on 'em that belonged to Fiji and Hong Kong and New Zealand and the Empire 'as it then was.' Sounded great to me. I may try it myself. Number two collected hammered coins, has list of stolen. Number three collected copper heads of Victoria like your friend Merton. Number four specialized in Henry VIII. One hit. I told him we'd be out this morning. He's expecting us."

"Good," George said. "I got two hits and two complete misses. My number one had a huge collection, apparently, and was trying to get every coin the English put out no matter when. Number two was trying to get all the kings that appear in Shakespeare's plays. Number three didn't answer, and number four was suspicious of the

120

whole thing and wouldn't discuss it at all, good-bye. I could hardly blame him. So we've got four live ones, right? Mine are expecting us too. Crighton, would we dare borrow your car for this expedition?"

"You most certainly cannot!" she said. "I am going to petition Brother Brooks for the day off. You have a very clear homestretch look about you, sir, and I intend to be in on every one of the last few minutes. Old Lady Ferrar should be there by now. You two just sit tight while I make a few administrative phone calls," she said, and disappeared.

Carson sighed. "This is what happens when you give them the vote. McKinley said we'd live to regret it."

By nine fifteen they were on the Parkway heading for their first stop with Crighton firmly behind the wheel. The nearest "victim" to the Minerva Club turned out to be a retired general in Chevy Chase. The house was enormous, baronial, and built in 1910, so it had a well-lived-in look. The general proved to be much younger than Crighton thought retired officers ought to be, but, as Carson later explained, this was because she did not know about up or out regulations. They outlined their mission inside the door and the general expressed easy hospitality and led them to a combination den and sun porch.

"Find yourselves a seat and I'll get my records," he said. He returned with a steel file tray that was loaded with cards, which were in turn divided by guide cards like a library catalog. "Here're my holdings. The ones that were taken have paper clips on 'em."

"What is your specialty again, sir?" George asked.

"The whole British series, actually. I started a long time ago— back in the war—World War II, that is. I started by trying to get a coin for each sovereign, and then when I'd gotten most of those, I thought I'd try for one example of every design that'd been done, then every *kind* of coin, and it all just got bigger and bigger."

"How many English coins are there?" Carson asked.

"Well, Seaby's identifies over 3,500 without getting into moneyers and mints."

"And you have all of them?"

"Oh hell, no. I'm barely halfway along . . . well, maybe two-thirds, but I've got more to get than I have years to get 'em in. And the new prices have just about driven me out of the market."

"How many coins were stolen?"

121

"About a hundred—but they were my prize specimens. That's why I had them at home, of course. I was going to lecture on 'em the next night at the Cosmos Club."

Crighton asked, "Do you—or did you—have a groat of Richard the Third?"

"Let me see." He flipped cards as one would look for books in a card catalog. "First, Richard . . . then groats . . . yes, there were only two made. One in London and one in York. I had the London. It was among those that were stolen."

"What kind of information do you keep about them? Do you know how much you paid for it?"

"Yes. Seven hundred dollars."

"When was that?"

"I seem to have purchased it in 1962. Bought it at the bourse at the ANA convention that year."

"What's a bourse?"

"That's what we call the buying and selling that goes on at a coin convention. There's a separate place with tables and things set aside for people to trade. I bought the groat from a man named Barrow."

"What!" Carson shouted. "Paul Barrow?"

"Yes. Do you know him?"

"We do indeed. Do you know him personally?"

"No, I've never seen him before or since."

"And that was one of the coins that was taken?"

"Yes, do you know the coin?"

Crighton broke in. "Does your card show the mint mark of the coin?"

"Yes. There are only two, as I recall. Richard struck so few. I think you've got a choice of a sun rose or a boar's head. Maybe a lis. I'd have to look it up. But mine was the rare boar's head."

"Holy Mother," said Carson, and seized the top of his head again.

"Does your card tell anything else about it?" George asked.

"Only that the coin was in 'very fine' condition and was from the London mint."

"Well, sir," said George, "you have been most helpful. There is just one more thing to be asked. You've caught us a bit off guard with the knowledge that you bought the coin from someone we know. We really ought to see if any of the other coins that were stolen were purchased from the various people we've met. Could we prevail on your patience to examine the cards with clips on them to see if there is any linkage?"

"No problem," the general said, "but unless you particularly want to see the cards, why don't you let me search them. A hundred cards . . . it might take the better part of an hour. Why don't you give me the list, and I could call you if I find any. Would that be of any help?"

The three looked at each other and agreed. "That would be wonderful. Let me give you the names and a place to call me . . . just leave a message, if I'm not back yet . . . and we'll be much in your debt."

The arrangements were made, gratitude expressed, and in five minutes they were on the interstate beltway heading for Annapolis. By ten thirty they were back at the Werner-Bok, exhilarated but confused. The Annapolis collector had proved to be a small-time dealer who sold U.S. coins, but who saved English hammered pennies for himself. He had an extensive collection of silver pennies—exclusively pennies, in fact, except for a single coin he had purchased from a man he had met at a coin show at the Smithsonian in 1962. The coin was a rare groat of Richard III that the man was selling, and ordinarily he would not have gone outside his penny specialization, but the chance was too good to miss. The seller was a foreign service officer about to leave for Europe. Name of Barrow. The coin was among those stolen.

An English literature teacher at the University of Maryland in College Park had lost his collection of the coins of the Shakespeare kings. He had had a single coin of Richard III. It was a so-called boar's head groat and had been purchased from a man by the name of Barrow in 1962. It had been the rarest one in the teacher's collection and none of his coins was insured. A search of the records of his thirty other missing coins showed no further linkage with the Gadsby Tavern club.

The fourth name had apparently left for work by the time the three arrived, so they turned around and headed directly for the library. En route they agreed on the next stop. Carson would go to the stored intelligence of the Werner-Bok and Crighton would drive George to see Alexa Lehman. They parted grimly with a sense of foreboding. Each in his own way was fearful of what they were going to find.

123

15

STEVE CARSON ENTERED THE REFERENCE department testing his research options. Books via the card catalog; digital tape via the CRT. He leaned toward the cards as an old friend and found himself hoping that he would not have to use the computer—the impersonal acquaintance. Now there's a weird attitude, he thought. The CRT was fun to play with—sort of like a pinball machine. You punched in the letters like you flipped the ball up to the top and then you sat back and watched what happened as the screen filled or the ball bounced back and forth on the way to the bottom. But you didn't take either one seriously. My God, he thought, you'd better take the computer seriously. It was sucking up half the money of the campus budget and would probably keep someone from hiring him someday. I wonder if the stupid thing is really worth it?

He was now at the catalog and thought with a chill, They're about to close this thing down and we're stuck with the computer whether we like it or not. Would it really be a loss to future scholars or was he simply old-fashioned already? A reactionary at twenty-seven? Thank God he was born when he was. He looked at the banks of trays, so comfortable, so efficient—and so familiar. He forced himself to focus his thoughts. Counterfeiting. Fakes. Forgeries. Coins—Fakes and forgeries? Best try counterfeiting first.

He tried the proper trays, discovered a handful of books to his delight, and selected the latest three. He copied down the necessary data·on as many call slips and passed them in at the desk. Ten minutes later he had one book and two crumpled slips marked "Not on Shelf." Par for the course, he thought bitterly. Back to the old shotgun approach. He returned to the card drawers and filled out twenty slips and began to cycle them through the system three at a time, while reading whatever the exercise produced.

By the end of an hour, he was feeling less hostile and more arrogant. Knowledge is power or something, he thought. Another pair of legs walked down the aisle, and following years of careful conditioning he swept his eyes from heels to waist whereupon this pair stopped and turned toward him.

"Good morning," she said. It was the angelic Miss Arnette. "What's new in the coin department?"

"Lady, if you knew you would weep."

"Then why don't you tell me and we can feel bad together."

Carson had the sense he might have misjudged the librarian.

"Can we talk here? I assume all these scholars are cataleptic, but there just might be one doing some creative thought."

"Come into my office."

With reluctance he ignored the straight line, and accompanied her into a glass-walled cubicle even smaller than Crighton's room in the basement below. He draped himself down a folding chair beside her desk, and brought her up to date on the cumulated excitement of the day and a half since they had parted before a dead computer terminal.

"So you see, it's been coming across the plate faster than we can handle it," he concluded.

"And what are you after this morning?" she asked.

"Counterfeits and forgeries. We're pursuing the thought that there may be more of these Richard groats than chance would normally put into one community. There may be nothing wrong with them at all. It's just possible that this guy Barrow had a really narrow specialty: he saved Richard the Third boar's head groats

125

and he was cashing in his investment. That would explain their entry into the market, but not quite explain why Eleanor was pitching 'em in among her stationery."

"You think he was fencing counterfeits?"

"Fencing, yet? You watch too much television. Maybe fencing. Maybe even making them himself. That's what I was trying to run down. What's the percentage and how is it done?"

"And what have you learned?"

"The following. You are prepared to make notes? Questions will be asked."

Miss Arnette had the grace to laugh and made herself comfortable.

"We are discussing the counterfeiting of silver coins here. Copper isn't worth it, and the faking of gold is incredibly tricky. But silver. Not bad. I'm going to give it serious thought myself if I blow the thesis.

"The first bit seems to be casts. Here you take a good coin and pour plaster or plastic around it, split the sides, remove the coin, put the sides back together, and fill it up with melted metal. Aberration one: if you're trying to make money on the metal, you use lead or a cut mixture of silver, and pick up a percentage on the debasement. Defense? You weigh a real coin versus the suspect one and they won't match. Apparently there are books that tell you what the real coin should weigh too.

"Aberration two: in casting it's murder to get rid of the bubbles. When you pour in the hot metal, it congeals before all the tiny bubbles can float off. Defense: look at it under a microscope. The holes show all over if it's done sloppily, and in the fine details if it's done carefully. Technological breakthrough here. The bubbles can be much reduced by putting the mold in a jeweler's centrifuge like they use to make fake Indian bracelets or bridgework. You spin the hot metal and squeeze the bubbles out. Or. You put an electromagnet on both sides of the mold and let the magnetic field squeeze the bubbles out. This was invented by an Egyptian mechanic—of all unlikely people. The mold bit tends to be a little soft—unsharp—in the design part, but you don't notice it if you claim it's wear. Or trust the seller."

Carson loosened his shoes and Miss Arnette said, "You've shaken my confidence already. There's more?"

126

"There is. 'False dies' is the phrase in art. You simply . . . simply? What am I saying? It's hard as hell to do, apparently, but murder to detect. You 'simply' make a new die . . . anvil . . . yourself, slam a newly cast or rolled piece of silver in it with a sledgehammer, and you've made a coin your very own self. Jewelers and engravers apparently do the dies for the gold pieces that are worth thousands, but hammered coinage is the poor man's Elysian field. If a ham-handed Saxon who didn't even have bifocals much less a jeweler's loupe could do it, so, by God, can we. The more I read the more I want to try it."

"Do these look real?"

"They are real. That's the trick bit. When they're new they're too shiny, but apparently a week in a bottle with a rubber band and two weeks in a pan of mud on the back porch does wonders."

"Do you really mean a rubber band?"

"I do. Did you ever drop one in with your Mother's sterling? Turns it black and you black and blue if she finds out who did it. According to book 4-B, it's the sulfur used in the vulcanizing process."

"Murder."

"Oddly enough, precisely."

"How common is this?"

"False dies?"

"Forgery in general."

"Apparently it used to be limited to gold and rare classic coins. U.S. gold coins have all been forged for years—from the twenty-dollar piece right down to the single buck—which is a damn small coin, I gather! I was delighted to learn that the most famous German forger—who made impeccable dies for Greek and Roman coins—was named Carl Becker. Hah! Carl Becker is my idol. He was president of the A.H.A. and spent a lifetime at Cornell. Had the most beautiful writing style of any historian we ever produced. His essay 'Everyman His Own Historian' is the absolute alpha and omega of my trade."

"You're sure it was a different man?"

"I hope not, but I'm afraid they never met."

"So the increase in value makes it worthwhile counterfeiting anything now?"

"You got it."

127

"Then how does the ordinary woman protect herself against all this . . . stuff?"

"Ah. If I'm reading those things right, weighing and microscopes seem possible, but they require too much knowledge at the first. After you get to be an expert you can cover yourself, but what do you do while you're getting smart? Apparently the answer is 'buy from somebody reliable.' Which, of course, is the old authorized dealer pitch that every product uses. But I don't see any way around it here. Incidentally, if we're to believe all those books out there, even the dealers don't really weigh and look. What *they* rely on is the coin's history. If they know where it came from and who had it last and where it was found, et cetera, et cetera, they buy and sell without question. Maybe the old hands know what the things *should* look and feel like and spot oddities just by the general sense of things."

"So how do you relate all this to your own troubles?"

"Good question. I was just approaching it when your lovely . . . your arrival . . . distracted me. So let's try it together. May I free associate, doctor?"

She smiled and nodded gracefully. "And what do *you* think it means, Mr. Murgatroyd?"

He laughed. "All right," he said. "We know that Barrow sold a bunch of thousand-dollar coins around town. Apparently he could do this because he looked respectable, maybe he's known around the community as a longtime member of that highly respectable coin club. Are the coins he sold counterfeits? We won't know until we get our hands on 'em. If they are, has he been doing this with other coins? Is this where his capital comes from? Possibly. How can we find out? Have to work on that. Any chance that that whole club is playing this game? Possible . . . but unlikely. Unless they're incredibly good actors, they seem to have too many tensions flowing back and forth between them. Too many social levels. Too much contempt. Then just one bad apple? More likely. What do you think?"

Miss Arnette frowned and said seriously, "It's more exciting the way you say it, but unless you know something you haven't told me, you're relating an awful lot of activity to . . . to what? Just five duplicate coins in Eleanor York's table drawer? You're assuming too that they're some way related to the other two or three you

128

found in the stolen collections. But you're only relying on probabilities—the unlikely probability that this rare coin would turn up in so many places. But beyond that you have no reason to think that there's any relationship among them." She stopped and looked thoughtful.

"You do take the color out, Madame Librarian."

"Well, what I'd be afraid of is that you've let the color distract you. Just because the coins are strange and somewhat exotic, you've assumed that they are what's behind the robberies and the murders. What if the murders were the old-fashioned result of greed or jealousy or infidelity or something—you'd have let the coins completely distract you. Have you really thought out the traditional motivations? Could somebody have blinded you—deliberately—with all this gold and silver?"

"Money, booze, or sex," Carson said wryly. "That's what Conrad keeps reminding us—Conrad's the police type. 'Don't get too fancy.' Hmmm. Occam's razor. Let's go back and start over."

Miss Arnette nodded primly and let her pupil proceed.

129

16

CRIGHTON," SAID EDWARD GEORGE, "YOU handle this Washington traffic with great skill. You know the myth is that Washington traffic is the worst in the world. That isn't true. It's simply the worst in the Western Hemisphere. There is nothing wrong with traffic here that after you've driven it for five years you can't cope with. The only problem is the four years while you're learning. It's not impossible, just suicidal, that's all." She had just completed crossing four lanes of traffic while going around a fountain-filled circle left-handed. "My God," said George, "can I open my eyes now?"

Crighton laughed. "You shouldn't have any trouble with these things. You're an Easterner where the streets are all slanty anyway. The people Washington wipes out are the tourists from the West where all the streets are either north and south or east and west. Do you know why all our avenues are on the diagonal here?"

"Something to do with L'Enfant, but I can't remember what. How does it go again?"

"Right. When L'Enfant was laying out the Washington street pattern—in a swamp, you remember—the French Revolution was going full blast and the only way the Parisian troops were keeping order was to set up cannon at the main intersections. They could shoot down the boulevards and keep the rebels divided by neighborhood. L'Enfant is supposed to have laid out the diagonals so the cannon fire would be neater, and he put in the little circles where the diagonals met so they could set up the cannon without stopping the traffic flow."

"Marvelous. Well, he certainly stopped the traffic flow for the visiting tourist."

"Didn't do much for the government employee on a snowy night either."

"Verily."

They crept past ten long black limousines parked three deep in front of the Indian Embassy and started up Massachusetts Avenue.

"Did you warn Madame Lehman we were coming?" Crighton asked.

"Yes, and she sounded genuinely eager to see us. Remarkable woman. I wonder if she's with us or against us."

"You've seen more of her than I have, but . . . I find the running antagonism between her and Eleanor the most interesting. Have you noticed it?"

"I have, and I agree. You'd have thought Alexa would have pictured Miss York as a younger version of herself—attractive, independent, poised. I wonder what the subtle difference is?"

"It is real, isn't it? There's no chance they're really allies and this needling is put on for our benefit?"

George laughed. "You're getting as bad as I am. I've gotten so I don't trust any of that distinguished Committee any farther than you can kick a bass drum under water. Odd. What time is it?"

Crighton looked at the dashboard clock and said, "Nearly eleven." The preeminent question, Are you going to make it? was left unasked. Depending on how you figured it, either he had one hour to bring it off, or none. He did not volunteer his views and ten minutes later they were seated in Alexa Lehman's living room with the civilities exchanged.

131

George accepted a cup of coffee and said, "Madame Lehman, I think we are almost finished."

"Do you know who has done these things?" she said with astonishment.

"I rather think I do, but I want to nail down a few details before I take any action. I guess the nails are in place. Possibly cleat their ends is the image I want."

"Why, that's marvelous! Splendid! What are you going to do about it? What can I do to help with the . . . confirmation?" Crighton could not tell if she was simply saying the expected words or if she was genuinely pleased with George's news.

"We stumbled over an odd element last night," he said, "and I would be grateful if you would tell us what we should think about it. It is a simple little detail and may have absolutely nothing to do with the savage actions that brought us all together. But . . . as far as we know, at this very moment there are five silver coins lying casually, loose, in a drawer at one of the homes of the original Executive Committee. We understand they are what is known as Richard the Third boar's head groats. By the way, what is a groat?"

"A groat, as I recall, is four pence," she said. "There is no such coin in my gold series, so my memory may be faulty here, but I think it's like saying, 'five pennies make a nickel, five nickels make a quarter,' and so on. Four pennies make a groat, three groats make a shilling, five shillings make a crown. I suspect the word came from the French *gros tournois,* a medieval French coin, but I'm not sure by any means."

"Bless you. Now, if you were visiting one of these homes and pulled out a drawer and saw five of these groats looking back at you, what would you think?"

There seemed to be no recognition of the incident or coin. She simply replied, "I guess I'd be a little surprised to see any antique coin treated so casually, but I don't think I'd sense any overtones."

"Would the fact that they were Richard the Third's startle you?"

"No, I don't know that much about English silver. All my coins are gold, you recall, and I have never studied the British silver series. Are Richard the Third's rare or common? Let's see, his gold coins are practically nonexistent. Ah, I suppose that's because he was in for such a short time—and probably his silver would be equally rare. No, five of his coins would be unusual."

"But this is not common knowledge?"

"There really is no common knowledge in coin collecting. Each series has its own idiosyncracies. Each must be learned. It's all a matter of rarity and demand. I remember Mr. Merton once telling me in great triumph he had gotten a copper penny of Queen Victoria that was worth a thousand dollars—1860, it was. I recall thinking that solid gold sovereigns of about that date were selling for less than a hundred dollars apiece. It's impossible to generalize."

"Ummm." George looked directly at her and thought reflectively, There is no evidence that she knew anything at all about those coins before I brought it up. She seems to sense nothing dramatic in the incident. What is the significance of this? Could the significance be there is no significance to it at all? He smiled to himself and said, "Alexa. Forty-eight hours ago, you called me and got us involved in this. Since then, a second person has been killed, and I am going to do my best to see that a third is incarcerated for the rest of their natural lives. If you'd known then what you know now, would you have played it as you did?"

"Without question. I was right. You've done just what I wanted you to." She said it firmly in the tone of two friends confiding in each other.

George looked back at her thoughtfully, and said, "I wonder. Do you know who did it? And why?"

"No, I really don't. I just knew that I was not going to let some muddle-headed bureaucrat put the tragedy in a file drawer and forget about it. Justice had to be done."

"Ummm. Can you come to the clubroom at the Tavern at two this afternoon?"

"Of course."

"Good. I'll see you there." He rose, looking oddly irritable, and motioned for Crighton to join him. Five minutes later they were headed for Georgetown University.

"Dr. Charter, it was good of you to see us." They were in the young professor's office, a high-ceilinged room in one of the antebellum, gray stone buildings of the Georgetown campus. The windows were long and narrow, and the walls so tall that one had the sense of wishing to lay the room on its side—which would have doubled the floor space.

"We won't take but a moment," George continued, "but I need your reaction to an oddity in our survey."

133

Charter said stiffly, "I think it is only fair to be absolutely candid with you, Dr. George. I am not in sympathy with any of your activities and I do not wish you to think I am helping you interfere in this quite private matter."

"May I point out to you, sir," George said without rancor, "that this private matter has cost two people their lives and may soon cost more. You will recall that when murder trials are conducted the case is not brought by the aggrieved family, but by The People versus . . . Murder is everyone's business."

Charter looked surprised. He hesitated a moment and said, "I accept your point. Also I am curious about your—what did you call it—oddity? You may proceed."

Crighton thought, God, what guts. Steve would have apoplexy.

"Thank you," George said with a slight smile. "Yesterday we were going through the home of one of the original Executive Committee and pulled open a drawer to find five Richard the Third groats lying loose among the papers therein. My question, sir: Is this unusual? Does it in itself merit our attention or thought?"

Charter narrowed his eyes and looked slantwise at the two. Crighton thought, He's more interested in what's behind the question than he is in the incident itself. There's no evidence of his being familiar with the coins or the background to the query.

"I don't see what you're getting at," he said flatly. "Five duplicate coins might be unusual. I don't know how rare that particular piece is. It wouldn't be hard to determine. North's book assigns rarity to all strikes."

"Could we find out how many of that coin have been sold in the past, say, ten years? In rare books there are auction records published every year. Is there something similar in coins?"

"No. In the English series—I am interested only in the crowns of the British mints—most coins are bought and sold in England. Baldwin's, Seaby's, Spink's. There are American dealers but I have found them to be overpriced, reluctant to buy back the coins they have sold you, and in general rather arrogant."

Crighton thought, Whoops! If *he* thinks they're arrogant . . . !

"Could we ask the various dealers if they had sold any of these coins and to whom?" George asked.

"I would doubt it. Our participants are so fearful of theft that we reveal next to nothing to anyone."

"How much buying and selling is there among collectors—outside the trade channels?"

"Quite a good deal. We keep trying to get better and better specimens—or we did in the past. As the coins got more valuable and there was increasing demand for them, we all became reluctant to give up what we had—now we mostly add on to our holdings. One of the results is that there has been more buying from estate sales and less trading within the group."

"But if one of you tried to sell your coins to others in the area or at a convention, it could be done?"

"Oh yes, if the person was known and established. You couldn't rent a motel room and advertise in the paper for a one night stand." He smiled as if to congratulate himself on the clever thought.

"Dr. Charter, I am asking the various members of the committee to join me at the Gadsby Tavern clubroom at two o'clock. Would you be good enough to meet with us?"

"No, I don't think I can afford the time."

"Dr. Charter," George said in a startlingly cold tone, "I tell you flatly you should be there to protect yourself and your interests. My invitation is not casual. Good day, sir." George stood up and, motioning to Crighton to join him, walked out of the room without looking at Charter again.

They met Paul Barrow sitting on a bench in front of the Carlyle House in downtown Alexandria. The reconstructed building was glowing like a newly worked sampler. The antique house was white, the grass brilliant green, colorful flowers lined the red brick walks. Barrow was gray. He gave the sense of a black-and-white picture set in a technicolored scene. He started to rise when they approached and George motioned him back down.

"No. Sit there. We'll join you."

A second bench sat at right angles to the one on which Barrow had waited, and George and Crighton shared the vacant one.

"What a magnificent building," George said. "It says 'Carlyle House.' What's a Carlyle House?" He looked toward the center of interest that looked like a James River plantation with the traditional wings cut off.

"Brother Carlyle was a penniless Scotch clerk who got fat rich around here about 1750, married one of the Fairfax girls, and built himself that handsome house overlooking the river. When they organized the Braddock Expedition, it was the largest house in town so all the governors met there. If you count people, it was a great help to the Revolution—Franklin and Jefferson and John Paul Jones all stayed here. If you count governmental successes, it was about par with our own. They drafted a smart-ass letter in there that precipitated the Stamp Act, the Braddock campaign ended with him dead, half his troops unburied in the woods, and the rest running in a rout, the . . . Believe me. We're following in a great tradition around here."

George laughed. "Come now. Surely our batting average is higher than most societies."

"Then it's too bad we can't quit while we're no further behind than we are."

"If you had your career to do over again, what would you do differently?"

"I'd claw and scratch to get as much power as I could, if only to keep some other clown from getting it, and then I'd govern right out of Calvin: man is inherently evil and institutions are designed to keep the damage we do to each other at a minimum."

"I'm sure you're wrong," George said ruefully, "but it's getting harder and harder to prove why."

"Yes," said Barrow.

"Sir," said George more seriously, "we could use your help in a matter. We've been talking to various people in the area who had coins stolen and we came on two items of interest. First, a pair of them had Richard the Third groats among their missing materials. My first question, then, is: are these coins fairly common or are they rare?"

Crighton, who had been half-watching tourists go in and out of the Carlyle House, slowly turned her head to look at George. His half-truth was a new approach. What was he thinking of? she wondered.

Barrow seemed distracted by the question. His eyes darted about the scene and when he started to speak his throat was full and twice required clearing.

"No," he finally got out, "no. They're quite common. Richard the Third was really fairly modern, you know—he came just before the Tudors. No, there are many of his coins about."

136

"Good. The other question is related to you. One of the coins had been sold by you. Do you remember it?"

"One?" Barrow cleared his throat again.

"Yes. Had you sold more?"

"No. Well, possibly two. How did the person know I had sold it to him?"

"He had remarkably detailed records."

"And none of the others did?"

"Apparently not in such detail."

That is a barefaced lie, Crighton thought. What is he up to?

"When was this sale?" Barrow asked.

"I don't recall—the man may not even have . . . no, I think it was in the early sixties."

"Yes, I may have sold some coins then, it was probably when I was cleaning out everything but my specialty. About then I unloaded everything but my Roman things." He cleared his throat again.

Mr. George lies much more easily than Barrow does, Crighton thought. But Barrow has much more to lose. She wondered where George was headed, but she was quite unprepared for the approach he actually took. George began to look very concerned and his speech became increasingly formal.

"Very well, if that is the way you remember it, I think we need not waste any more time on it. Mr. Barrow, I believe I know what has happened in this tragic matter in the past two days. I believe you do too. I suspect you have given it a great deal of thought, and I think you will agree that it would be best if the matter were resolved, should we say, as a body? Could you join the remainder of the group there at the clubroom at two this afternoon?" He nodded toward Gadsby's Tavern, which was barely a block away but hidden by Alexandria's antebellum city hall.

Barrow looked down and sighed. "I'll be there," he said quietly.

"Thank you," George said almost harshly. He motioned to Crighton and the two started back to the garage where the Audi had been parked. As they walked along the uneven bricks of the old town, George spoke as if preoccupied by other things. "That'll get him to the meeting, and that's the important thing for now."

137

17

WHEN CRIGHTON AND GEORGE RETURNED TO the Werner-Bok, they found Carson in Crighton's office seated at her desk and surrounded by five-by-eight note cards. They literally covered the surface of the desk, papering the flat and roofing the standing books and in-boxes.

"Am I the only one working in this outfit?" he complained. "Here I am, grinding the head to the bone, while you two wander about goofing off and clogging the streets."

George laughed. "You've got all the trappings of the martyred employee. We're guilt-ridden already."

"You can sit beside your desk, woman," Carson said. "If I'm the only one doing anything constructive anyway, the least you can do is give me the furniture to do it on."

Crighton dropped into the side chair, and said, "For the first time in his life he's driven to make a little effort, and he's insufferable.

138

We've been out chivvying Comrades Lehman, Charter, and Barrow. What've you been up to?"

"Yes," said George, "we await your report."

"And you shall have it!" He gave the grand gesture and began. "Working in reverse order, I just hung up from your lovely friend, Miss York. She in turn has heard from Comrade Charter and understands that you, sir, are planning a convocation at the Tavern this afternoon. Charter assumes that you've invited everyone, and York assumes that surely you've been trying to reach her, but to save you any further trouble be it known she will be present at two as she's sure you want. Do I detect a faint concern about protecting her interests, or is it really my body she's after and she's using this excuse to mask her desire?"

"My God," said Crighton. "The mind boggles."

"I am delighted that Miss York has saved us a call," George said. "I wasn't sure how I was going to bring that off. Professor Charter seems to have done it for me. He does seem to keep Miss York abreast."

"Leave it alone, Carson," said Crighton.

He grinned and continued, "Previous to the Beautiful Eleanor, I heard from your friend Conrad, sir." Carson dropped a note card reminding himself of the York call into the wastebasket and picked up two recording the Conrad call. "The Lieutenant would have you know the following: one, they have checked out five sets of handcuffs. The first four were bought at a security outfitter on Route 50 in Arlington. They're the real thing. Cost twenty-two dollars apiece. Anybody walking in off the street can purchase them. Most of the store's business is to watchmen and building guards. Their sales slips on across-the-counter transactions simply list the item, so they have no address or description of the purchaser. Dates they've got, but it was always two or three weeks before the murders. Set five was bought in a magic and novelty store on Pennsylvania Avenue across from the Federal Trade Commission. They're nothing but glorified toys, made in Japan, distributed by just that one store in the area. Most of the store's sales are souvenirs and the stuff goes to visiting high-school kids. No idea of who or when these were purchased."

Carson dropped a card into the wastebasket and read from the second one in his hand. "Re bullets. Three of the wounds were made

139

by a small caliber handgun of the type that can be purchased off the sidewalk on Fourteenth Street for twenty-five to fifty dollars—depending on the time of night you make the transaction. The fourth was by a .22 caliber target pistol of the variety you can get at most Virginia sports stores. No sales of same in the local area for the past month."

"Was the .22 from the same murder as the off-brand handcuffs?" Crighton asked.

"It was."

"And, of course, it was the Merton death."

"Exactly."

"Was the Vandermann murder among the other three or four?"

"It was."

"Wow!" said Crighton.

"I agree," said George. "Could be very significant."

Carson dropped the second card into the wastebasket. "Zilch on alibis and car to date. That's all Conrad's news."

"When we finish here, don't let me forget to invite the Lieutenant to our meeting," said George. "There is some merit in asking him to take me so we can enter together." George stared at the ceiling for a moment.

"We turn now to the counterfeiting matter," Carson said. He picked up the note cards in sequential order until he had reduced them to a single, serial pile. "Whilst the following data came from almost two dozen sources, I have integrated it as follows." He made a final adjustment, and noted, "By the way, Jones, I'm going to give you just ten more years to marry me, and if you haven't made up your mind by then, I'm going to throw myself at the feet of that angelic librarian up there. Behind those big blue eyes of Sister Arnette there operates a very sharp mind. Legs aren't bad, either. Hurry up. I'm not going to wait forever. You're down to your last decade. Re the counterfeiting of coins . . ."

His audience leaned into him, both concentrating intently on his report. It was twelve o'clock. Either way you calculated it, George's forty-eight hours were up.

18

TWO HOURS AND FIFTEEN MINUTES LATER George was on the sidewalk looking up at the third floor of Gadsby's Tavern. Lieutenant Conrad was at his side and, he hoped, everyone else would be waiting in the room above. He wanted the timing crisp.

"We're going up there?" Conrad asked.

"Yes. Third floor. No elevator. And don't ask if I think I should. I've been through that before and why not? Come on. Slowly but steadily."

George reentered the colonial doorway and started up the stairs—hallowed by the footsteps of the Founding Fathers according to Steve, George recalled. This time there was no one waiting at the top landing, and George led Conrad down the hall and into the clubroom. A quick glance told him everyone was there. No one had taken a seat, everyone was standing, and the dynamics of territoriality struck George as having potential significance.

141

On one side the three young people were together, Crighton, Eleanor York, and Carson. Miss York was wearing a plain, unornamented dress, which in repose simply looked stylish. However, when she made even the slightest movement, it dramatized if only briefly a plane of hip, thigh, breast, or shoulder. Steve was profoundly distracted, and Crighton grimly amused.

Madame Lehman was standing at the opposite side of the table paired with a shattered Barrow, and George thought wryly of Crighton's earlier comment, Barrow's the pitiful one, he's *really* vulnerable. Barrow had the look of a man who had taken a make-or-break chance and lost. There appeared to be no further fight in him. Madame Lehman was looking directly at George—indeed she was the only one who seemed willing to look him in the eye. She was dressed in an obviously designer inspired outfit, like Eleanor's, plain, appropriate for an afternoon at a museum, but highlighted by tiny threads of gold. Planned or happenstance? George wondered.

Robert Charter was standing alone at the end of the table. He was oblivious to Eleanor York's attractions and was watching the Lehman-Barrow alliance with single-minded intensity.

"Good afternoon," George broke the silence. "Thank you all for coming. May I suggest we be seated." As they arranged themselves around the long table he identified each to the lieutenant who acknowledged the successive introductions with a nod—from a distance. George seated himself almost stiffly, remaining in a commanding, authoritative posture.

"We are here to resolve this tragic situation," he said. "Three days ago, at approximately this time in the afternoon, I met Karl Vandermann for the first time. I found him pleasant, interesting, and concerned. It appeared that he had convinced himself that a trusted member of his Executive Committee was determined—indeed had promised—to kill him. He asked for my assistance to prevent this.

"The following evening Steve and I went out to Professor Vandermann's house to discuss, among other matters, this frightening threat. I must admit, Dr. Vandermann's attitude toward his danger was so casual, so almost cavalier, that I was not certain whether his concern was real or simply symbolic—literary? I was therefore doubly horrified to arrive at his house and find him dead."

George turned to the police lieutenant. "You will recall that we

142

found him sitting in his study chair, at his desk, with his arms manacled behind him. He had been killed by a single shot, precisely in the center of his forehead."

George returned his attention to the larger group. "At Madame Lehman's urging, I set out to determine who had killed Professor Vandermann, and I believe I now know who did it. Then to my horror, within twenty-four hours of Vandermann's death, Jerry Merton was killed. I believe I know who killed him too. I am staging this rather dramatic way of telling you about my conclusions because I am not absolutely certain I am right. I need your help. I think that several of you know fractional, unrelated facts that you can provide me when you see the total picture. I do not expect much help from the murderer. I hope to have it from the rest of you. I remind you: two members of your group are dead. I think I know who killed them. Tell me, am I right? I believe the following."

George himself appeared at ease, leading the group deliberately, almost grimly through his thinking. His audience sat absolutely motionless around the table, following his thoughts with total attention.

"Mr. Merton needed money. He had failed to acquire it through the more accepted means, so he set out to steal rare coins—a value he knew and could control. As I had originally concluded—and all succeeding data confirmed it—his method of operation was to examine the incoming announcements of various fellow club meetings in the metropolitan area, identify those involving English coins, and select those whose meeting dates fell on Saturdays or Sundays—forcing the participant to remove his coins from the usual safe deposit vault before the close of business Friday."

George turned toward the lieutenant and said, almost as an aside, "He would approach the victim's home after dark, dressed in unidentifiable clothing, force them at gunpoint to their studies, and after handcuffing them to a chair, collect the family silver—and casually, the coins. Three of the victims either refused to reveal where the silver and coins were, or recognized Merton, and he shot them. His natural sense of order, apparently learned in a lifetime of lining up columns of accounting figures, led him to order his crimes in a precise, repeated, and almost symmetrically controlled manner."

His attention returned to the group as a whole. "All this has been observed and confirmed. We move to the first unknown. The thefts had been proceeding smoothly. There was not the slightest evidence that he was suspected by any of the various police jurisdictions through which he skipped about, but for some reason Dr. Vandermann must have begun to suspect him. Why Vandermann? The police had not even identified a repetitive pattern in the community. Did Vandermann? Were some of his friends victims? What would have occurred to seize Vandermann's attention? Alexa, can you help on this?"

"No," she replied. "I don't know *why*, but I agree that it occurred. Karl said to me his heart bled for someone here who was tearing himself apart over something and taking a great risk."

"Did he actually say 'tearing *himself*'? "

"Yes."

"Ummm. Therefore male. Another thing: the implication was that these transgressions gave Vandermann pain as well as the offender. Would he have felt so bad about *Merton's* fall from trust, faith, or loyalty? None of the rest of you had the slightest respect for him."

"Karl met him in some way years ago and always felt sorry for him—a there-but-for-the-grace-of-God thing, I suspect. His attitude toward Jerry was an almost literal 'more to be pitied than censured.' Knowing how Karl felt about him, I tried to be somewhat more charitable myself than is my usual wont." She smiled wryly.

"I can't tell you *why* either," Eleanor York said, "but Dr. Vandermann had made the same comment to me about his disappointment and his distress."

"Ummm," George continued, "that corroborates the next step, but does not tell us what got his attention. Very well—the next step was when Steve and I arrived and he told us that he had been trying to solve a problem involving his Executive Committee and he had apparently succeeded too well.

"By that night, Saturday, apparently Merton had become completely convinced that Vandermann knew, and he was about to be exposed. He must have had two choices. He could assume that Vandermann knew who was doing it, but—since he had not yet told the police—he might not yet have told anyone else, in which case the quicker he was killed the better. Or, he could assume that Vandermann had told someone already, in which case he was probably doomed anyhow, but with the prime witness dead, he might be able to bluff it out. Either way, it was worth the chance, and he would be better off with Vandermann dead. He re-created the other silver robberies and what at first appeared to be an unfortunate interruption by Steve and me was in fact an even firmer corroboration—witness—of his attempted staging. The Fairfax police were in fact taken in and all was well.

"But he tripped his own destruction. He brought the knowledge of the other robberies into his own club—the one community he had rigorously avoided until now."

George paused and looked at what remained of the Executive Committee. Barrow had sagged even lower in his chair and was staring at the center of the table in front of him. Alexa Lehman was watching George but her eyes were completely flooded and as George looked at her the first tear overflowed and ran down her carefully made up cheek. The tear hung on the edge of her jaw and she made no attempt to remove it. Charter sat slightly sidewise in his chair and attempted an imperial look in response to George's examination, while Eleanor York frowned and appeared to be trying to follow George's exposition and to anticipate where he was going next.

George took a breath and started to speak, but before he could express his first word, Paul Barrow turned his head toward him and said in a low, tired voice, "I think you've dragged this out as far as you need to, sir. You are right, of course. I doubted if I could get away with it, but it was worth a try. I killed Merton. I really had no choice, and God help me, I have no remorse whatsoever. You figured it out from the Hunchback's groats, didn't you?"

George nodded.

"They're counterfeits. Did you know that?"

George nodded again. "We were reasonably certain."

"I sold them around the area myself and . . . you said you had found one person who knew his coin came from me. Was he really the only one?"

"No. We have tied at least four to you already."

Barrow nodded without either surprise or apparent resentment. "I assumed so. No, when I learned that Merton was doing the robberies it was obvious that all those duds I'd sprayed around fifteen years ago were coming back together in one place. You'd have had to be a lot stupider than Merton was not to realize they were fakes—you don't get that many rare coins in one place and each exactly like the other without figuring out what's going on.

145

You said he had two choices about killing Karl." Barrow laughed bitterly. "I had two too. As soon as he figured out what was going on, it wasn't going to take much effort to find out from someone where they came from and then it was either exposure or—considering his ethics—more likely blackmail for the rest of my life. Either he'd already told someone, and I was already down the tube, or he was going to, and I'd better beat him to it. He'd tried to make Vandermann's death look like the others. I thought I'd try to add *his* to the series—another coin robbery."

"But you're an especially moral man. How could you execute him without . . . what was your word . . . remorse?"

"He was guilty! I'd worked it out just like you had. Somebody had to kill him—ought to kill him. With the way justice has deteriorated in this country, he'd probably have gotten off scot-free on some goddamn technicality. I just saved the state the cost of trying him."

"Where did you get the coins?"

"He had them all. I put the gun to his head and he told me where they were, hoping to buy me off. I shot him just as dead."

"And how did they get into Eleanor's drawer?"

"I put them there when she wasn't looking. I was planning to pick them up when the pressure was off. She knew nothing about any of this."

"Why didn't you simply dispose of them when you got them back from Merton?"

For the first time, there was a pause in the rhythm of his response. Finally, he said, "I thought I'd better keep them as insurance. In case they caught me for killing him, I'd have proof that he was blackmailing me."

"You'd claim."

"Yes."

"And where did you get the counterfeits in the first place?"

". . . Abroad . . ."

"No more specific than that?"

"There's no need to drag anyone else down with me. Anyway, the poor son-of-a-bitch is probably long since dead."

George chewed slowly on his lip looking directly at Barrow. Barrow looked back, tired, a beaten man. George shook his head sadly, and said, "Very well. You were right, I'm not sure the judicial system is tight enough these days to hold you either, but

146

I'm going to try. You say you killed a man without remorse. I am going to urge the lieutenant to arrest you and I will see you are tried, and while it may not be simple, I will try to see that you are found guilty and that you spend the rest of your life in prison. At your age I should think that will finish you. Your contacts with your peers will be ended. Your freedom. Your reason for life. Was it really worth it?"

Barrow looked slowly at each of the remaining members of the Executive Committee. Lehman, Charter, York. He stared directly into the eyes of each participant. "Yes," he said quietly.

George too looked at the group and then said harshly, as if in final judgment, "And have you all anything to add to this tragedy that will see justice served? Dr. Charter?"

Charter was a chastened man. His natural arrogance was gone, and he looked like an awed adolescent witnessing events far beyond his control. "No, sir. Nothing. It is all horrible."

"Alexa?" George asked.

She shook her head. She seemed totally unaware of the tears forming and running down her cheeks. "No, nothing," she said softly. "It doesn't seem real. No."

"And you, Miss York? Have you anything to add to this account that would serve justice?"

She looked directly at him and shook her head, "I have nothing to add," she said firmly.

George threw himself against the table in front of him and said harshly, "Have you not! You should. Indeed you should, for of all the people in this room you know that what he said is a pack of lies." He looked at Alexa Lehman. " 'It doesn't seem real,' you say— the reason it doesn't seem real is because it isn't!" He stared furiously at York again, who sat half-smiling, slightly pushed back from the table. "Would you sit there without a word and let him take the blame for this? What is it? Is your contempt for him so great you can see him destroyed without a flicker of shame? Your contempt for men? For everyone but yourself?"

The remainder of the group sat transfixed, stunned by George's clear fury. He explained more quietly, "I am convinced what really happened is that the professor was killed by Merton just as I described, but as we sought his killer, Miss York watched us not only identify Merton, but learn his most detailed crimes. She sat at my side and watched first the computer then our research reconstruct the events that led to this disaster. She quickly realized that all too many of the robberies involved collections into which Barrow here had sold her counterfeits. Yes, *her* counterfeits. Steve's research revealed how jewelers can fake antique jewelry by their centrifuges—but dentists use exactly the same instruments to make precision crowns and bridgework. Crowns. Dental and numismatic. Their products are equally metallic, detailed, mold mark and bubble free. This young lady took a single Richard III groat, no doubt made duplicates on the self same dental centrifuge she uses at work, seduced this poor man into using his respectability and his credentials to sell the counterfeits, and I suspect to give her every dollar of the profits. God knows how many she did and the extent of her exploitation . . . I suspect Mr. Barrow was so dazzled by her appeal that he could be talked into anything."

"No!" Barrow shouted. "It was just as I told you . . ."

"It was not. She killed Merton with a dispassion you cannot even conceive. She has used you for years." Barrow started to speak and George raised his hand. "Don't waste your chivalry on this young lady, Mr. Barrow. She is as hard as her dentals. Furthermore, it will do you no good whatsoever. I suspect Lieutenant Conrad here will be able to trace the purchase of those anomalous handcuffs to her, probably tie her movements to Merton's apartment house, and find gunpowder in her clothes. I would be surprised if the remainder of the coins she stole from Merton will not be traceable to her house or her safe deposit boxes. There will be other elements to be pursued as well."

"Try to prove it," she said coolly.

"I intend to, madam. I certainly intend to do that very thing. Lieutenant Conrad, the young woman is yours. I believe she murdered Merton in your jurisdiction, and Merton was a citizen under your care. Either way, she is your responsibility."

"Yeah," the lieutenant said. He looked at Eleanor York who returned his stare defiantly. "You stay right where you are. But about this . . . this . . . him." He pointed to Barrow. "He says he did it. Did he do anything?"

"Probably not for fifteen years. You're going to have to see when or if he gave up selling fake coins for her, but the murders? Nothing."

"Then all that . . ."

". . . was in his mind as it was in mine. We both figured out how it *could* have been done. She knows how it *was* done, since she did it. When we verify the truth, they will be the same."

She laughed, apparently at ease. "Oh, let's not get uptight about it. The counterfeits simply acted as income transfers—Madame Lehman will tell you how useful they were to the community. Kept everybody liquid and moved the cash from the haves to the have-not: me. The community won't be much better off without Merton, but it sure won't be any worse. Who'll even know he's gone? A nothing if there ever was one."

"Miss York, the crime is murder, not the assignment of social value."

"Get off it. All this crap about the worth of the individual. Who are you kidding? Nobody matters. How many people do you know that you'd really feel sorry about if you never saw again? One? Two? I doubt even that. You might be mildly interested in whatever happened to . . . but do you really *care?* We're like ants. You can stomp us out and what difference does it really make to anyone? We tell ourselves stories to make us feel wanted. No. Get it while you can. Get it for yourself. You *owe* it to Number One."

She looked at the other members of the Committee with wry contempt and then said directly to George, "No doubt there are some left who share your idea of justice and morality. Personally, I think it's a bore. You notice I do not admit to any of the nonsense you've been putting out here, and believe me, I do not expect to spend a single night in confinement over this thing."

Conrad raised his head sharply. "Oh, really?" He straightened up very deliberately and struggled to his feet. "Not one night?" he said. "I think we'll be able to do better than that." He looked toward George and smiled slowly. "Amazing," he said, "you've done it again." He shook his head and turned toward Eleanor York. "Now," he said, and jerked his head toward the door. "You are under arrest. You have the right to remain silent. You are not required to say anything or to answer any questions. Anything you say . . ."

149

19

LOYAL TROOPS, YOU'RE ON YOUR OWN TIME and my conscience," George said. They were settling themselves around Alexa Lehman's elegant coffee table and the silent maid had appeared with baroque tray, silver service, and pastries, as if she had eased out of an Edwardian engraving. "Alexa, I made a pact with Steve and Crighton here that if they'd give me forty-eight hours of their thoughts, I'd promise to resolve the Vandermann irresolution. My promise and the contract ran out at noon. I am three hours illegal, overdrawn, and overdue."

"And we are awed," said Carson. "By God, you came closer than I would have thought possible. I am now prepared to throw myself on that paper of mine with a cleansed mind and a renewed faith in facts."

"Speaking of facts," George said, "you two scooped them up with marvelous speed and efficiency. What a delight to watch you work. I could not be more pleased—or more grateful."

150

"But dammit," Carson said, "it was an irritating solution. Would York really have let Barrow fry for her? That's outrageous."

"Yes," George said, "I'm afraid she would have done just that. I'm afraid she is totally ego-centered. Herself is literally all that exists for her. She would have let him evaporate from her consciousness with no more awareness than we do people we read about in last week's newspaper. I doubt if he was ever that real to her in the first place."

"But he was willing—forgive the cliché—to make the 'supreme sacrifice' for her. How can that be?"

Crighton said, "She may have answered that one herself. When I was there that night, she said that men were hopelessly romantic. Far more than women, she said. If it's true, she played it right. It's sad. Could Barrow really have loved her that much?"

George sighed, "Without question, I'm afraid." He looked at Alexa Lehman. "In spite of all our reputation, we men are essentially monogamous. In a man's lifetime there is usually one— just one—woman that is like no other. It may come at any time in his life stream, but that one locks into his soul and is the only one that really gives meaning and color and texture and edges to his life. It's wholly irrational. Why one? Why just one? There are a hundred million of you loose in this country alone and yet there will be just one who unplugs all the rational . . . all the . . . the . . ." He shook his head and lapsed into silence.

"Yes," Madame Lehman said quietly. "In Victorian times, it was supposed to be the woman who gave herself so completely. I think you're right. In ours it's probably the man. I wonder why? What made the difference?"

Crighton said, "If I may change the subject, what happens now— with York, I mean?"

"Conrad says he'll take it from here," George replied. "He says he has enough to work from. I'll check with him when I get back from England."

"Is the system tight enough to ensure justice?" Carson asked.

George frowned. "I don't know. We can only hope."

"I'm not so pessimistic as you all are," Madame Lehman said. "The 'system' is sorting itself out. There's a basic quality . . . fiber . . . to people that always appears when it's really needed. Don't you think the pendulum is swinging back? About everything. Aren't the structural elements firming up again?"

151

"I tried that on Dan Boorstin when I was in town the last time," George said. "He's not only the Librarian of Congress but a Pulitzer prize historian of long renown, and he says that the idea of the 'pendulum' is a myth. He claims it never goes back. He says history is totally a matter of 'moreness.' Sometimes you get lots of more and sometimes more comes slower, but you never go back. Nothing is ever undone. Technology . . . inventions never disappear. Inflation is never erased. Taxes never really go down. Laws never evaporate. Government . . . intolerance . . . national memory . . . I do hope he's wrong."

"Enough of this!" Madame Lehman said. "You should be standing on a peak of triumph. Rational thought has succeeded again. Justice preserved!"

"Yes!" Carson said. "Everything works out for the best. Madame Lehman, tell this beautiful but confused woman here that she should marry me and quickly. We are wasting time. Excitement, new experiences, bliss she cannot conceive are slipping past her every hour she is not at my side. Don't you agree?"

Madame Lehman laughed. "I do indeed. You make a persuasive case."

"Does he?" Crighton grinned and made a sweeping gesture of the opulent room. "I notice you've managed to tough it out alone for forty years."

"I was simply waiting for one good enough to share it with." She smiled and cocked an eyebrow at George. "Edward, I was intending to give myself a week in Salzburg at the end of the month. Why don't you let me show you the Old Country after you finish that London thing of yours? It'll do you good."

"Why, why . . ." George had a slight sense of things slipping through his fingers again, but he hesitated only a moment and then said, "Why not! The affairs of men taken at the flood . . . I'll do it."

"My God," said Carson. "Our leaders have no difficulty in making up *their* minds. Crighton Jones, why do you? Let me remind you of the case. Given: you should marry me and now. Reasons? One: . . ."

They all laughed and George thought, Not the pendulum. Not the cycle. The helix. Round and round. Always the same. But getting better and better, higher and higher on every loop. He smiled. The good stuff never tarnishes. Bright and shining, every day like a Florentine florin—or maybe a ducat of Venice. He wouldn't miss a minute for the world.

152